Flo —
I hope,
I had f
I'm still writing book 3 —
Demeter's Daughter, so hang
in ther ☺ Beth

Artemisian Artist

The Goddess Series
Book One

Beth Mitchum

Don't settle for less than the
best for your life.
Beth Mitchum

Windstorm Creative
A Lavender Line Book
Port Orchard • Seattle • Tahuya

Artemisian Artist (The Goddess Series, Book One)
copyright 2000 by Beth Mitchum
published by Windstorm Creative

ISBN 1-59092-339-1
9 8 7 6 5 4 3 2
First edition March 2006

Cover by Buster Blue of Blue Artisans Design.

For information about film, reprint or other subsidiary rights, please contact Mari Garcia at mgarcia@windstormcreative.com.

The Lavender Line is a series by Windstorm Creative, a multiple division, international organization involved in publishing books in all genres, including electronic publications; producing games, videos and audio cassettes as well as producing theatre, film and visual arts events. The wind with the flame center was designed by Buster Blue of Blue Artisans Design and is a trademark of Windstorm Creative.

Windstorm Creative
7419 Ebbert Dr SE
Port Orchard, WA 98367
www.windstormcreative.com
360-769-7174 ph

Windstorm Creative is a member of Orchard Creative Group Ltd.

Library of Congress cataloging-in-publication data available.

Dedicated to
Artemis
the Goddess who refused
to marry and settle down.
She chose instead to roam the forests
with a band of nymphs.
Way to go, Artemis!

Ode to Artemis

Artemis, O Artemis,
Ever Goddess of the Moon.
Artemis, O Artemis,
Your dark time cometh soon.
Your arrows wound me,
I am often felled.
Your oceans move me,
Tides within are swelled.

Artemis, O Artemis,
Ever Goddess of the Night.
Artemis, O Artemis,
Swift of foot, quick to flight.
Your wonders amaze me,
How you effect a change.
Your powers grace me,
Seem no longer strange.

Acknowledgments

Thanks to Windstorm Creative for launching the Lavender Line to make a home for lesbian fiction. A great big thanks goes to Jennifer, Cris, and Natalie for editing and advising on the original edition of *Artemisian Artist*. A big hug and kiss to Buster for doing such an awesome job on lay out and for the cover for the new edition. You are a patient man.

Thank you also to my readers. I've enjoyed the feedback from the people who matter. You can keep track of my forthcoming books through my web site at www.ultravioletlove.com. I'd also like to thank my family and friends for their encouragement and my animals for their company while I write. I want to thank my customers in the Waldenbooks stores where I've worked for the past twelve years. You're great, and I'd think that even if you didn't buy my books. Warm and hearty thanks to those Waldenbooks managers who got my books in your stores and helped me to sell them. You are great people and I'm glad I got to be part of this elite group for a while. I miss those annual manager meetings. No, really... I just miss you folks!

I'd also like to thank Ginny for being who she is and for sharing her uniqueness with me.

Artemisian Artist

The Goddess Books

Beth Mitchum

Chapter One

As I staggered down the hospital corridor, I questioned the wisdom of trekking through the hospital parking lot at five o'clock in the morning. Darkness still cloaked the city for even the Sunshine State of Florida is subject to the lengthening of night as the winter solstice approaches. Although it was early December, it had been a warm day, and the night was not much cooler. Dark, low-lying clouds had kept the warmth of the day from dissipating and at the same time hinted that a storm was approaching.

When I arrived the afternoon before, I had not concerned myself with finding a parking spot in a well-lighted area, since I had planned to stay at the hospital throughout the night. Relieved at discovering that my father had finally fallen into a sound sleep, I seized the opportunity to escape the clutches of the hospital chair, which had been my roosting place for the past nine hours. All I could think about was going home to sleep in a real bed.

My father had undergone surgery the afternoon before, and I had volunteered to act as family nurse to help him through the first night. It seemed logical enough at the time. My oldest brother, James, lives in another state. Stanley, my other brother, lives locally, but has a traditional nine-to-five job that requires clarity of thought and attentiveness. My younger sister, a high school student, had to attend classes the following day.

As a freelance artist, I keep late hours as a normal course of my work. Inspiration usually ambushes me around nine at night and doesn't ease its grip until three in the morning. Consequently, I was the only realistic choice for the job of nocturnal baby-sitting. That's how I came to be half-walking, half-stumbling through the hospital corridors in the wee hours of the morning.

Upon entering the elevator lobby, I caught a glimpse out of the corner of my eye of a figure dressed in hospital blues. Since I was at the hospital, this was a phenomenon not worth thinking about twice, so I stepped into the elevator and turned around to punch the appropriate buttons. As I looked sleepily through the narrowing gap of the closing doors, the figure in blue surgical scrubs turned around, looked right at me, and smiled.

Momentarily forgetting my fatigue, my mind alerted my eyes to get a good look while I had the chance. Meanwhile the figure had bent down over a red plastic bag, according me a pleasant view of a nicely rounded bottom. Without notifying the rest of my body of its intentions, my hand suddenly jerked up and pressed the "Door Open" button. The doors abruptly reversed their course and reopened. As much surprised by this action as I was, the woman stood up and looked at me, color rushing to her cheeks.

"Um, did you want to get on this elevator?" I asked, realizing too late how incredibly stupid I must've looked.

"Oh, I, thank you, yes," she said, scooping up her belongings and racing across the hall to the waiting elevator. "My lunch bag split apart, so I was just putting my food into a plastic bag until I take my lunch break."

I glanced at the translucent red bag in her hand. "You put your food in a bag that has 'biohazard' written on it? I suppose that must be in compliance with the new food labeling laws. You must eat some serious junk food."

Looking embarrassed and slightly offended, the woman in blue said, "I don't eat junk food. Not much anyway. It's just an apple, some potato chips, and an egg salad sandwich."

"And a Snickers bar," I added with a sly smile.

"Okay, yeah, and a Snickers bar. But it has peanuts in it."

"And sugar and butter."

My companion folded her arms across her chest and turned to look at me with a puzzled expression on her face. "Who are you anyway, the nutrition police?"

"No," I said tiredly, "I'm sorry. It's past my bedtime, and I'm afraid my mean sense of humor is showing itself." When the elevator churned its way to a stop at ground level, I punched the "Door Open" button again and motioned for her to exit ahead of me. "Beauty before beastly."

My companion in blue laughed, her eyes sparkling at me with just a hint of surprise in them. "Oh come on. You're not that bad!"

I stepped out behind her and started down the hallway, oblivious of my whereabouts or destination. "Sure I am. I just insulted a hard-working nurse at five in the morning. If that isn't beastly enough, let it stand then for my appearance. After dozing all night scrunched up in a chair, I've got to look beastly at any rate."

"Good heavens! Why were you sleeping in a chair? And I'm a doctor, not a nurse."

"My apologies, Doctor. My father had surgery today. No, make that yesterday. I stayed with him all night to make sure he was going to be okay."

"There are cots available for overnight guests."

"Oh, nobody told me that. Perhaps the nurses had heard rumors about my vicious wit and thought that I deserved to sleep sitting up."

"Perhaps," the doctor relented with a slight grin. "Herniated disk?"

"Excuse me?"

"Your father. Does he have a herniated disk?"

"Yes. How did you know that?"

"I'm assigned to the wing you were just in. I know why all those patients are there. Only one of the surgery patients could pass as your father. Higgins, right?"

"Right. Of course you wouldn't have just guessed. I thought for a moment that you were psychic."

She laughed slightly and smiled. "No, I'm definitely not psychic, which means you will have to tell me your name."

"Elizabeth Higgins."

"Not married then?" She asked with a barely discernible lift of her right eyebrow.

"No I'm not, though lots of married women retain their family names these days."

"True enough. So where are you heading, Elizabeth Higgins?" She asked after we had walked quite a distance down a long hallway. "Home for some shut-eye?"

"Yeah I guess, although I don't know if I'm heading in the right direction. I'm afraid I just started following you. I figured you knew where you were going. Where is the visitor's parking lot anyway?"

"Back the way we came, I'm afraid. But why don't you let me get you some coffee? You look as though you could use it."

Glad to prolong the conversation with this gorgeous woman, I readily agreed, even though I'm not overly fond of coffee.

"Here's the coffee shop." The doctor waved her hand in the direction of an open door. "Cream or sugar?"

"Cream," I said, walking into the deserted lounge.

The doctor pulled a crumpled dollar from her breast pocket. She carefully unfurled the bill and attempted to iron out the wrinkles on the edge of a table. Then she gestured towards one of the four tables in the sparsely furnished room. "Pick a seat while I get your coffee."

I glanced around the room and winced at the heavy-handed use of cadmium yellow in the decor. It was way too bright for my tastes, especially at this hour of the morning. But I had to admit that it made me feel a bit more awake, even if it did clash with my T-shirt, which was more of a burnt sienna shade of rust.

I sat down and watched as my companion inserted paper money into the change machine. She scooped up the quarters from the change cup and slipped them into the coffee machine's coin slot. As soon as she pressed a couple of buttons, the machine whirred into action. A few seconds later she lifted the clear plastic door and removed the steaming coffee cup from the machine's mouth.

"Here you go," she said, as she handed me the cup then turned back to the machine. She stepped to one side of the machine, blocking my view of the buttons. This time she pushed three buttons instead of two. I smiled to myself as I deduced that she must have been adding sugar to her coffee. "So, are you working the night shift?" I asked, realizing too late what an asinine question it was.

"Actually I'm working a 72-hour shift. I'm in the middle of my residency, so I get to work all the truly crappy hours."

"Do you get to sleep at all?"

"Sure. I can go to the back room in the doctor's lounge and crash on a cot. There's a very loud intercom speaker in there. I can usually grab a couple of hours of shuteye during the night without missing an emergency summons."

"How on earth can you live like that? I keep late hours, but I still have to get at least six hours of sleep. Otherwise I turn into a real bitch."

With a mischievous laugh, the doctor asked, "I see. And what kind of bitch are you when you do get your needed rest?"

Startled by her wit, I burst out laughing. She did the same. It probably wouldn't have been nearly as funny if it hadn't been so far past my bedtime.

When she stopped laughing, my coffee companion said, "I sure hope you don't have to go to work today. You look rather wiped out."

"Thanks for the compliment, but no I don't have to go to work. I'm a freelance artist. I usually work late into the night then sleep until ten or eleven. I'm not usually awake when the sun rises. We have an agreement. The sun doesn't look at me when I get up, and I don't look at it when it gets up. I'm afraid I'm a night-owl by nature."

"I'm not sure what I am by nature. Adaptable I guess, which sure comes in handy in the medical profession. I can sleep in any position at any time of the day or night. I simply adjust to my environment. Perhaps that makes me a chameleon."

"Hmm, you don't resemble a chameleon in the

slightest. Most chameleons I've met don't have such engaging dark eyes."

My doctor friend smiled. "And just how many chameleons have you been introduced to lately?"

Applying my best poker face I answered, "Oh, lots. But none who were doctors."

Her only response was a low chuckle.

"So, Doctor, do you have a name, or does everyone just call you 'Doctor?'"

"Hell yes, everyone calls me 'Doctor!' I worked hard for that title, and I have yet to tire of hearing it. But you can call me Dr. Terri."

"Cute," I said under my breath, before taking another sip of coffee.

"What did you say?" Dr. Terri inquired with that little lift of her eyebrow I was rapidly growing fond of.

"I said, 'cute,' meaning you or your remark actually. Though that's not to say that you're not cute." I shook my head. "Oh never mind." I made a mental note to kick myself later for that stupid response. I was far too tired to carry that task out at the moment.

Dr. Terri smiled again. As she took a sip of her coffee, she closed her eyes and mumbled, "Mmm. Max sure knows how to make good coffee. I can feel the caffeine seeping into my bloodstream."

I looked at her curiously. "Who's Max?"

"The coffee machine, of course. That's what we call it."

"Any particular reason why?"

She shrugged her shoulders. "Oh, I suppose there was a reason at some time or another, but I have no idea what it was. I'm a recent acquisition to this hospital. I just picked up the name from the other hospital staff. Most of us go out of our way to use this particular machine. For some unknown reason, it makes the best cup of coffee in the whole place."

"I see. I thought for a moment when you closed your eyes and started mumbling about Max making good coffee that you were remembering a lover of yours."

Dr. Terri leaned back in her chair, stretching out her long, slender legs. She looked at me from beneath her dark brown bangs and said, "No, I would definitely not be recalling a lover named Max." As she started to take another sip, she said, very quietly, something that sounded like, "Maxine, maybe."

"What was that?"

She shook her head slightly. "Nothing." After another sip of her coffee, she looked out from under her bangs again. "So were you worried that I had stolen your boyfriend Max?"

"No. I definitely wouldn't have a boyfriend named Max."

"Don't care for men named Max?"

I laughed lightly. "Something like that."

By this point in the conversation, I was definitely getting the feeling that we were both sending out tentative feelers. Surely the woman who sat next to me was a lesbian. Or at least I sure hoped she was. When she closed her eyes and savored a quiet moment, I took a good long look at her.

She was about 5'8" to my 5'6". A little on the lean side, but definitely not emaciated. She had just enough padding in all the right spots. Her dark brown hair was cut in a style reminiscent of a pageboy, making her look like a throwback to an earlier decade. She opened her eyes and returned my scrutinizing looks from behind the cover of her bangs. Her eyes were a rich van dyke brown.

I tried to pull my thoughts together. I wanted to believe that her flirtatious manner indicated that she was as interested in me as I was in her and that the spark I was experiencing was real chemistry between us and not just my overactive imagination. However, I was acutely aware of the fact that I wasn't operating on all circuits. It had been a long day. I was tired and sleepy. It could be that my wishful thinking was misinterpreting her words and expressions, and that the spark was merely the result of a little faulty wiring in my mental breaker box.

The silence that fell on our conversation was nearly oppressive after the light badinage. When I could stand it no longer, I ventured hesitantly, "Well, I suppose I had better find my way to the parking lot. I'm sure you need to get back to work."

Rising slowly from her seat, Dr. Terri smiled at me. "Yeah, I do need to get back to my wing pretty soon. I hope the coffee perked you up enough to get you home. How far do you have to drive?"

I got the distinct impression that Dr. Terri wasn't quite ready to end our conversation so I walked slowly back to the elevators. "Only about ten miles or so. I live on the south side of town."

Dr. Terri's face lit up. "Really? So do I, if you could call it living. I really live here. I just check in occasionally at Sandy Lake Villas."

"I'm in San Juan, around the corner," I interjected quickly.

"What do you know? We're practically neighbors. At least, we would be if I were ever home. I really don't know anyone around there, since I'm gone so much."

"Well, if you ever need someone to talk to when you are home, I'm in apartment fifty-seven. I'm usually awake until at least three, so it doesn't matter if it's late."

"Thanks. I might take you up on it. It isn't easy to find anyone who is awake at odd hours."

We were walking slower and slower, as though we both dreaded ending our conversation. Not knowing what else to say, I said, "Sorry again for my rudeness. Hey, you never ate your lunch."

Dr. Terri's face reddened. "Actually, I wasn't on my way to eat lunch. I was just coming down for coffee. My money was in what used to be my lunch bag, which got torn open on the corner of a cleaning cart. That's why I had to put it in a plastic bag."

"But surely you could have found a less conspicuous bag?"

"I don't usually run into anyone in the middle of the night. I didn't think anyone was going to see my bio-hazardous lunch."

We laughed again, a little nervously this time. After a brief pause, Dr. Terri stopped walking altogether and extended her right hand towards me. "It was nice to meet you, Elizabeth Higgins. I'll have to tell your father I ran into you. Are you coming back here later?"

I stopped and reached to shake her hand. As I gave her hand a quick squeeze, I felt a small jolt of electricity run up my arm. I pretended not to notice. "As a matter of fact, I will be back as soon as I get some sleep. I'm taking the day off from my work. Will you be here?"

"Yes, but I might not be very visible. I'm scheduled to assist in surgery, and I don't know when I'll get out. Maybe I'll see you in your father's room later."

"I hope so," I said, as I started walking again.

She accompanied me as far as the elevators then waved as I continued on. "Apartment fifty-seven?" She asked as the elevator doors were closing. "Yes," I said quickly. "Come over or call any time. My number is in the phone book."

I walked the length of the corridor to the exit. As I pushed the glass doors opened, I wondered what would come of this encounter. Lost in thought, I headed off in the direction where my car was parked.

Chapter Two

The morning sun found its way into the room through a crack in the curtains, waking me with a sliver of brilliant light. I realized immediately that something was amiss, though I couldn't quite figure out what it was. Then I remembered that sunlight doesn't penetrate my bedroom window like that. The mini-blinds and curtains I installed block out all morning light so I can sleep late.

Where on earth am I? The words, "What the…" escaped my lips as I tried to sit up to get myself oriented. Suddenly a streak of pain hit me like a two by four to the back of the head. "Damn!" I quickly laid my head back on the pillow.

A voice that sounded just like my younger sister's said, "Liz? Are you okay?"

Totally disoriented, I opened my eyes. "Melissa? How did you get into my apartment?"

She giggled her charming adolescent giggle. "Silly, I'm not in your apartment and neither are you."

"Where am I then? Is this a dream? It definitely has a dreamlike quality to it. Except that my head really hurts. I don't usually feel pain in my dreams. What's going on?"

Melissa smiled and patted my hand the way our mother used to when we were sick. "You're in the hospital, Liz."

"The hospital!" My head pounded from my sudden outburst. "What am I doing in the hospital?" I asked more quietly. "And why do I feel as though the back of my head has been used for batting practice?" As a figure in blue scrubs came to the side of my bed, a weird feeling came over me. I recognized this person, but I didn't know why.

"What do you remember about this morning?" the woman in blue asked me.

"I, um, well, my father. I was at the hospital with my father because he had surgery. I stayed up all night with him."

The woman pulled a small flashlight from her pocket. "Do you remember anything else?" She spoke with a tone of authority and professionalism, yet there was a hint of personal concern hiding behind her words. She instructed me to look in various directions as she shined the penlight into each of my eyes.

When she turned the light off I glanced at the letters written over the left breast pocket of her scrubs. It read, "T. Jackson." I thought really hard, hard enough to make my head hurt even more.

"I remember drinking coffee with someone before I went out to my car to go home. Don't tell me I was in a car wreck! Is my Toyota all right?"

T. Jackson smiled warmly and reassured me that my car was fine and that I had not been in a car accident. Then she raised her right eyebrow and asked, "Do you remember anything else?"

When she looked at me like that, it all came back suddenly. "Dr. Terri," I said. "I had coffee with Dr. Terri. That's you, isn't it?"

Dr. Terri Jackson smiled warmly at me and said, "Yes, Elizabeth Higgins, I am Dr. Terri, your early morning coffee companion. Can you recall what happened after I left you in the lobby?"

"Not really," I said, feeling groggy. "I remember saying goodbye to you then heading out to the visitor's parking lot. That's it. Why am I still here?"

"Hmm. Well, my guess is that someone mugged

you this morning on your way to your car. A nurse arriving for the morning shift found you at a quarter to seven, about an hour after I left you in the hallway."

"Found me where?"

"You were crumpled on the pavement between two cars in the visitors parking lot. It was apparent that you had been robbed. There was nothing in the pockets of your jeans. No money. No wallet. Your keys were on the ground beside you. You weren't carrying a purse, were you? I don't recall seeing you with one."

"No, I never carry a purse. I always wear jeans with plenty of pockets. My wallet was in one of my back pockets, but apart my identification and various membership cards, I didn't lose much. I don't carry credit cards around with me. I had just a few dollars in my wallet and some change in my pockets. If they didn't steal my car, then they got away with precious little." I smiled weakly. "Unless..."

"Unless what?" Melissa asked, concern registering in her voice.

I looked at Melissa and then at Dr. Terri.

"I wasn't raped, was I?"

"No, thank goodness, you weren't," Dr. Terri said with sincerity.

I breathed a sigh of relief. "I can't believe I was mugged. Stupid mugger. I wasn't carrying a purse or anything of value. Incredibly stupid of him to pick me for a target."

"Him? Did you get a glimpse of your attacker?" Dr. Terri asked.

"I don't think so."

"So you definitely didn't see anything or anyone?"

"No, I didn't. I'm sorry."

"No need to apologize, Elizabeth. I just need to tell the policewoman, who is waiting outside for information regarding your mugging. In the meantime, I want you to rest, but try not to go to sleep just yet. Let the nurses know if you need anything. Your concussion is mild. We'll let you go any time you're ready, as long as you have someone to drive you home. But you may be a little dizzy yet, so feel free to rest for a while first. I'll tell your father you're okay. He's been very worried since they told him. He blames himself, I think, because you were here at that time of day."

I smiled again. "That sounds like dad. He's a big baby, but he's always babied us too. 'Do unto others,' I suppose."

Dr. Terri gave my hand a squeeze then left the room.

I turned to Melissa, who was looking at me strangely. "You were talking to dad's doctor just before you left? What did she say about him? Is there something else wrong with him?"

Then it was my turn to giggle. I didn't have the energy to laugh fully. Besides I was afraid laughing would jar my head into frenzied pain again. "No, Dad's fine. I was just chatting with Dr. Jackson over coffee. I didn't even know she was one of dad's doctors at first."

"You were chatting with a doctor at five o'clock in the morning?" She asked, visibly awed by my audacity at treating a doctor like an ordinary human being. Then she eyed me suspiciously, "So, are you going to go to bed with her?"

I tried not to laugh, but couldn't stop myself before a small chuckle rattled my skull, spreading pain signals throughout my head at a speed faster than thought. "Why, I don't know, Melissa. Perhaps I will. Why do you ask? Were you interested yourself?"

Melissa turned a pleasant shade of vermilion. "I'm not lesbian, Liz, you know that. I've got a boyfriend."

"I did too when I was your age. I didn't realize I was lesbian until I was nineteen. Even then I kept pretending to everyone else that I wasn't. You may follow in your big sister's footsteps yet."

Melissa colored again. "What are you trying to do, recruit family members?"

I grinned a very small grin. "Not hardly. I know everyone else in the family is monotonously heterosexual. I have hopes for you though. You're different."

"Thanks, I think," was her only reply. Melissa looked thoughtful for a moment then said, "So, are you feeling good enough for me to drive you home, or do you want to hang around and flirt with your doctor friend?"

"Well, I'd love to hang around and flirt with Dr. Jackson, but I'm sure she has work to do. So why don't you walk with me very slowly over to Dad's room? Then you can drive me to my apartment."

Melissa helped me out of bed, which I finally realized was located in the emergency room of Lakeland Regional. I wondered how Terri Jackson had come to be in the emergency room, when she was assigned to the fifth floor, where my father was recuperating.

As we got off the elevator, we ran into Dr. Jackson again. "Oh, good. I just left a message for you with your father. The police want you to come in at your earliest convenience to fill out a report on the mugging. The policewoman that was here was very insistent. I had a hard time keeping her out of the emergency room."

"Okay, thanks, I'll take care of it. So where do I go to pay my bill?" I asked, hoping it wasn't going to be very much.

"Oh, don't worry about that. The hospital doesn't charge people for getting mugged in their parking lot. It would hardly be fair."

"How incredibly humane," I remarked. "Thanks for your help. I hope I didn't keep you from your work."

"That's all right. I got someone to cover for me in surgery this morning when I discovered you had been attacked."

I winced as another streak of pain shot through my head. Apparently the mere suggestion of being mugged made it hurt.

"Still hurt?" Dr. Jackson asked, looking genuinely sympathetic.

"A little. Not much more than a hangover though."

"Ouch, that's bad enough. Did anyone write you a prescription for a pain reliever?"

"No, but that's okay. Some extra strength aspirin should take care of it. Thanks again."

"Sure. I didn't really do anything. I just happened to be around when you woke up."

"How did you know I was in the emergency room anyway?"

"I had just gone down for my lunch break when I overheard a couple of nurses talking about the need for more security. I asked them what happened, so they told me that a woman had been attacked in the parking lot early this morning. I realized that it must've been you because there wasn't anyone else hanging around at that time. So I went to ER to get the full story. That was right before you woke up.

Good timing, huh?"

At this point in the conversation, Melissa must have gotten tired of being treated like a fence post. She shifted her weight to the other leg and cleared her throat. Her movements caught my attention, and it struck me that she had been awfully quiet. I glanced at her out of the corner of my eye. She was smiling a small, knowing smile, her eyes sparkling with mischief.

Mm hmm, that girl is definitely interested in all of this.

Addressing Dr. Jackson and Melissa, I said, "I guess I should check on Dad, so I can go home with a clear conscience. Will I be able to go to sleep when I get home? Or do I still need to stay awake?"

"It's a mild concussion, so it's highly unlikely that you'll slip into a coma since you're awake now. If you had stayed unconscious much longer though, you probably would have awakened in a regular hospital room. But your neural functions seem to be okay. I think you'll be all right, so go ahead and get some sleep once you get home. You must be exhausted, considering you were up all night. Is there anyone who can stay with you for awhile?" She addressed this last question in Melissa's direction.

Melissa piped up. "Yeah, sure. I can do it. I've already missed most of school today anyway. I can miss a little bit more. The school knows where I am, so I won't get into trouble. I have to be at work at eight tonight though, so I'll have to leave by seven."

"That'll be fine. She should be much better by then."

Dr. Jackson gave Melissa's arm an appreciative squeeze. Melissa smiled a radiant smile that revealed much more than simple enjoyment at being noticed.

Unless that bump on the head had distorted my ability to read body language, I was certain that Melissa was attracted to Dr. Jackson.

Maybe having a lesbian younger sister wouldn't be so great after all. What if she starts stealing all my girlfriends? Melissa is homecoming queen material. I'd never stand a chance with her around. I decided not to worry about it unless it became apparent that I had good reason to. For now, Melissa was operating under the guise of a heterosexual teenager, so I was relatively safe at the moment.

Melissa and I walked to Dad's room. We found him in good spirits, which had to be attributed to the painkillers. Dad has absolutely no tolerance for pain, so I knew he couldn't be in a good mood right now on his own strength. Not wishing to be around when the effects of his medication began to wane, we left after a few minutes.

Melissa stopped at a burger place on the way home, since she knew she would not get any junk food at my house. It never ceased to amaze me how someone with such horrible eating habits could have such a good complexion and a great body. Of course, she's on the track team at school, so that accounts for being able to metabolize all the fat and sugar. Sometimes I wished her face would break out or that she would gain twenty pounds, just so she'd realize what all that garbage would like to do with her body, which is exactly what it would do to mine.

Don't get me wrong though, I really love my little sister, even if I am a bit envious of her. She's very kind and compassionate. Now that she's grown up anyway. She was a real nuisance when I was in high school. I could never be sure I wasn't being overheard on the phone or that my letters weren't being read.

That's one of the drawbacks of having a sister who is so much younger. Her nosiness is how she became the first one in my family to find out I was lesbian. She found a love letter from a girlfriend in the pocket of a jacket she borrowed from me without my permission. When she read it, she was very confused and started asking lots of questions. She's been asking them ever since.

When we got to my apartment, I took a shower, put on an oversized T-shirt, and crawled into bed. I still felt a little dizzy, but that may have been due to a lack of food. I had not felt like eating anything, and at the moment sleep was a much higher priority. Yet as sleepy as I was, I was feeling too nervous and jittery to go to sleep right away. I got out a book, but managed to read only three paragraphs before I fell asleep.

Chapter Three

When I awoke later, the first thing I became conscious of was the ringing of the doorbell. I grabbed my alarm clock and turned the face towards me so I could see what time it was. My eyes wouldn't quite focus so I wasn't sure if the 6:45 were in reference to a.m. or p.m. Then I heard voices drifting back to my bedroom. One of the voices definitely belong to Melissa, but there was another one that was less distinct. The events of the day replayed themselves in my head, as the disorienting fog of sleep dissipated. I remembered why Melissa was in my apartment, but I could not figure out who else had showed up. I thought at first that it might be my brother seeking information about Dad's condition.

Then I heard Melissa's appealing giggle. "Of course," I mumbled, "It must be Robert. She probably called him to get a ride to work." Then I heard more female laughter. This time it was not Melissa's voice. *Oh, shit! That's Terri Jackson's laugh. What is she doing here? I bet I look ghastly.*

I eased myself out of bed as gently as possible. Just as I did so, I heard Melissa say, "I think she's still sleeping, but you can come on back to her room and check on her."

Before I could get back into bed or do anything to improve my appearance, the two women appeared in the doorway.

"Aha! Sleeping Beauty awakes," my sister said, gliding into the room ahead of Dr. Jackson.

I smiled at her then remarked sarcastically, "Sleeping Beauty, my foot. I probably look more like one of Snow White's dwarves."

I turned my gaze towards Terri. Before her eyes met mine, she briefly surveyed the total picture in front of her—my bedroom with its art studio look, my bed with its slept-in look, and my T-shirt-clad body with its slightly annoyed and rumpled look. When her eyes finally met mine, they were clearly registering bemused approval. She said with a smile in her voice, "You could pass for Sleepy well enough, I think."

"More like Dopey," I said, feeling disadvantaged by the situation, yet secretly pleased with Terri's approving survey.

Melissa giggled again. "Well, I need to get to work. Mind if I use your car tonight, Liz?"

"No, of course not. Keep it until tomorrow, if you want. I'm not going anywhere soon. Stan is staying with Dad tonight, since he can sleep in tomorrow."

Terri interjected, "I think I saw him as I was leaving. Your father is fine though. I doubt he'll need anyone to stay with him tonight."

"Good," I said, "one mugging in the family is enough for one week."

"Hopefully there won't be any more muggings. The hospital has assigned additional security for the weekend."

"I'm glad to hear that, though I think if someone wants to commit a crime badly enough, they'll find some way to do it."

Melissa cleared her throat. "I hate to interrupt this fascinating conversation, but I've got to leave now. I sincerely hope you two can think of something a little more interesting to discuss. Later, ladies."

On that note of rebuke, Melissa slipped from the room, barely suppressing the teenage energy that radiated from her body. A somewhat awkward silence followed in her wake. I suppose we were both busy trying to think of something more interesting to say. Shifting into doctor mode, Terri finally broke the silence with the old standby medical question, "So, how are you feeling?"

I laughed a small, nervous laugh, and said, "Well to be truthful, I'm feeling a little bit vulnerable just now."

Terri's facial expression changed to one of serious concern. "Because of the mugging?"

I laughed and shook my head. "No, I didn't mean that at all. I'm just not used to having a doctor in my bedroom. I had no idea you people still made house calls."

Terri's cheeks colored. "Sorry. I didn't mean to intrude. I just thought I would check on you. I knew your sister was supposed to leave at seven, and I wanted to be sure you were okay."

"Boy, you are one caring doctor."

"Actually it wasn't so much my medical technique that brought me here, as it was my maternal instincts. I really don't see you as my patient, since I wasn't the one who treated you. I didn't mean to make you feel uncomfortable. I can leave, if you'd like."

"No, that's okay. I think I could use some company right now, though I would think you'd be exhausted by this time."

"I'm okay at the moment. Of course, I can't guarantee I won't fall asleep in the middle of a conversation. Though I wouldn't sleep long. If you'd like, I could sleep on your couch tonight, so you don't get scared."

"I guess I might be scared right now if I could remember anything about this morning's attack. But

I can't. If it weren't for this bump on my head, I wouldn't believe it happened at all. So I'm not feeling traumatized or anything that dramatic. I just feel like talking. Can I fix you something to eat?"

"I haven't eaten yet, but you don't need to be cooking. I can call and have a pizza delivered. Does that sound appetizing?"

"Actually it doesn't. But, if you want to order it for yourself, that's fine with me. I think I'll fix something quick and easy like macaroni and cheese. It's kind of a comfort food for me. Shall I fix enough for two, or is your mouth set on pizza?"

"Macaroni and cheese is fine. Can I help?"

"Sure," I said very warmly, hoping we would soon be able to think of something more interesting to talk about. "You can grate the cheese."

"You grate your own cheese? I thought you said it was quick and easy. I was thinking more along the lines of something that comes out of a box with the letters K-R-A-F-T written on it."

"Okay, I'll grate the cheese; you can boil the water."

"I think I can handle that," she said with a warm smile. "Where's the kitchen?"

"This way," I said as I led her in the appropriate direction. "The Dutch oven is in the last cabinet by the fridge."

"The Dutch what?"

"The big pot you boil water in."

"Oh, okay. I guess you can tell I don't cook much."

"When would you ever have time?"

"Never, I guess."

Within thirty minutes we had our main dish and a garden salad on the table. My apartment is a small one, and the eat-in kitchen is little more than a breakfast nook. It made for a cozy dinner for two. Terri didn't seem to mind the close quarters. I know I didn't.

In spite of the awkward beginning, the dinner conversation flowed quite smoothly. I learned an awful lot about the medical field and life in a hospital. I daresay Terri learned a little something about an artist's life, albeit mine is a somewhat quiet and unobtrusive one. Her interest seemed genuine enough. She even expressed a desire to attend my next art show.

"So how much money does an artist make, if you don't mind my asking?" Terri asked, as we settled ourselves comfortably on the couch in the living room. I had fixed her some coffee and myself some peppermint tea.

"It varies. Last year, I made quite a bit, but no two years are alike. That's why whenever I have a profitable exhibit, I put as much as possible into certificates of deposit. That way I have something socked away for the lean times."

"Sounds like you have a good head for business too. Isn't that kind of rare in artists?"

"Stereotypically speaking, yes. We tend not to be a practical bunch. Somewhere in the gene pool, I managed to pick up a little shot of pragmatism, along with my creative streak. Of course, it doesn't hurt to have a brother who is interested in all that financial stuff."

"Well, it's always good to have a balance." After a short pause and a sip of coffee, Terri said, "My mother really pushed me into going into what she called a 'lucrative field.' She was afraid I would wind up where she did. She married my father when she was sixteen. He died suddenly when she was 26, leaving her with no money."

"That must have been very difficult for her. How did your father die?"

"He was a truck driver. His rig jack-knifed on an icy road in Colorado. He was killed instantly."

"I'm sorry. That must have been difficult for you."

"It was really hard on my mother, but I don't think it bothered me a whole lot. I cried at his funeral, but mostly I think because my mother was so upset. I didn't know my father very well, since he was on the road most of the time. I know him mostly through my mother's memories, which make him out to be a saint of course. I have no idea what the real Edgar Jackson was like."

"So how did your mother survive after that?"

"She did all right. I was an only child, so at least she didn't have more mouths to feed. It was rather lonely for me though, since she had to get a job to support us. I had to stay with neighbors every day after I got home from school. Mom worked as a waitress for seven years until she was finally promoted to assistant manager of the restaurant. By that time, I was in junior high. That's when my mother informed me that I was going to go to college, whether I liked it or not. With her promotion, she was able to begin saving money to make this dream of hers come true. It took a lot of scrimping, and a few scholarships and government loans, but we did it together. And now I'm working in a lucrative field."

"And are you happy?"

"I guess so. I don't really have time to think about it. Just about the time I start feeling lonely because I don't have time to make friends, I get called back to the hospital. It's a vicious circle, I guess. If I did make friends, they would have to be people who don't mind that I'm not around much. I'm not sure I would call people like that *friends*. They would be more like friendly acquaintances."

"How long will you be in this situation?"

"In residency? I have six months left. Then I have to decide whether I want to join a hospital staff, begin private practice, or throw away years of hard work."

"Sounds stressful."

"It is, I suppose. Not that I have the time or energy to worry about it," she said with a yawn. "Would you mind terribly if I crashed on your couch? My long hours are beginning to catch up with me."

"Of course not. Let me get you a blanket."

"Thanks," she said, leaning her head against the back of the sofa.

I went to the linen closet and pulled out a pale blue thermal blanket. By the time I returned with it, Terri had removed her shoes, stretched out on the couch, and was deeply into dreamtime. I covered her with the blanket then went to get one of the pillows off my bed. I chose the fluffiest one, plumped it up a bit, and then walked back out to the living room. Gently lifting her head, I slipped the pillow under it.

"Thanks, Mom," she mumbled in her sleep.

I smiled, wondering where Terri's mother was now.

Chapter Four

It was about 9:30 when Terri fell asleep on the couch. I went back to my bedroom with the intention of going back to sleep. Old habits are hard to break though, and I soon found myself at my drawing table. Picking up my sketchpad, pencils, and erasers, I tiptoed back to the living room. Sliding into my rocking chair, I sat down across from Terri's sleeping form. *I hope she won't mind,* I thought, as I began to sketch her likeness. *It's not often I find myself with such a captive model.*

For the next hour or so, I sketched, erased, squinted, and sketched again, in an attempt to capture Terri's attractive face. I lit several candles trying to prevent eyestrain, without disturbing my sleeping model. About the time I decided I was satisfied with my work, Terri moaned and turned over so that her back was towards me. *Nice timing,* I thought, as I gathered my supplies and carried them back to the bedroom.

I tried to lie down again, but still couldn't go to sleep. I made an attempt at reading, but could not focus on the plot. Finally I wandered out to the kitchen to fix myself some more tea. I snatched up the kettle before it could start whistling, as I had no idea whether my doctor friend was a sound sleeper. As the tea bag steeped, I leaned against one side of the doorway and looked out into the living room towards my sleeping guest. When I had decided that the herbs had steeped long enough, I tossed the dripping tea bag into the garbage can and glanced at the clock. It was 11:00 p.m. I wandered back out to the living room, teacup in hand.

I sat down in my rocking chair and began to stare in Terri's direction. She was lying on her back now with her arm flung across her forehead. After about fifteen minutes, the sleeping form said, "Want a picture?"

"What?" I asked in a hushed tone, wondering if she always talked in her sleep.

"Would you like for me to give you a picture? You've been sitting there for quite awhile staring at me."

"I thought you were asleep."

"I was. Now I'm awake." She sat up and looked sleepily at me.

"You didn't sleep very long."

"I usually don't after a 72-hour shift. I keep dreaming that I'm being summoned for an emergency. 'Paging Dr. Jackson. Room 511. Stat!'" She imitated an intercom-distorted voice.

"How terrible. Do you ever sleep more than a couple of hours?"

"Not unless I'm deathly ill. I just take a lot of naps."

"So you're awake now for awhile?"

"For awhile. Why are you still awake? Oh yeah, you're the night owl. What time is it anyway?"

"It's after eleven. I tried unsuccessfully to sleep. I just can't seem to fall asleep before 3:00 a.m."

"Is that coffee you're drinking?" She nodded at the cup on the end table beside my chair.

"No it's tea, but I can make some coffee for you. How many cups will you drink?"

"One is plenty unless we're going to stay up all night." She yawned and stretched her arms above her head.

"I wasn't planning on it, since I need to visit my

father tomorrow." I leaned forward, about to rise from my seat.

"The ever-faithful daughter."

"Not really. I don't usually have a lot to do with my family, except my sister. My brother Stan is a CPA. He lives in Tampa. James, the lawyer, lives in Chicago. Melissa wants to be a long-distance runner. She doesn't care much about what she's going to do to make money. She just wants to run. It's a passion with her, like art is for me."

"Where does your mother fit into all this?"

"Nowhere. My mother disappeared a couple years after Melissa was born. To this day, we still don't know whether she abandoned us, was kidnapped, murdered, or some other such thing. Although I suspect that James knows what happened to her."

"James is the lawyer?"

"Yes, and a damned good one at that. He knows how to keep his mouth shut. James was still in law school when Mother disappeared. That was in 1979."

"Why do you think your mother confided in anyone?"

I leaned back in my chair. "Two reasons. The first is the way James acted at the time. He seemed more tired than usual, but he didn't appear to be particularly worried. The rest of us were pretty much out of our minds with worry. The second reason is that I overheard James consoling Melissa about Mother's vanishing act. He told her that she was all right, but that she had to leave because it was too hard for her. I asked him about it later, but he said that I must have misunderstood him. I know I didn't, but it's useless trying to get that man to open his mouth about anything remotely connected to Mother."

"Do you have any idea why your mother would want to disappear?"

"I don't know. Maybe she got tired of taking care of everyone. My father was the youngest of four children. His three older sisters pampered him when he was growing up. They spoiled him rotten."

"So your mother had five children to take care of, counting your father?"

"Something like that."

"I can't say that I blame her. I know how hard it was for my mother to raise me."

"Mm, except that my Dad had a good paying job. It's just that he refused to do anything once he got home from work. After my mother disappeared, Dad hired a full-time housekeeper to tend to our needs. By that time, Stan and James were already grown. I was twelve; Melissa was two."

"There sure are some big gaps in your ages."

"Melissa and I were accidents. My mother didn't want any more children, but my father did. I remember hearing them argue about it once not long after Mom got pregnant with Melissa. It was always cloaked in humor, but I could tell that they were really fighting. The pregnancies were all difficult ones for Mother. She nearly died when Melissa was born."

"Maybe she got pregnant again and decided to have an abortion."

"I have wondered about that. Abortions were legal then, but I know my dad would have vehemently opposed her getting one, legal or not. He was raised Catholic, and even though he isn't a practicing Catholic, his upbringing influences him more than he cares to admit."

"Have you tried asking James about her lately?"

"No," I sighed. "I just figured he'd evade my

questions."

Terri leaned towards me. "Maybe not. It's worth a try anyway."

"Maybe."

"The worst he could do is not answer you. Sheesh, how did we get on this subject anyway?"

"You asked me about my mother."

"Oh, yeah. I had no idea it would turn into a tale of intrigue."

"It isn't that bad, is it?"

"Well, let's just say that I'm really curious now to find out what happened to her. I suppose it's too late to call James. Where did you say he lives?"

"Chicago. What time is it?"

Terri looked at her watch. "It's almost midnight here, so it wouldn't be quite eleven there."

"That's not too late. He stays up late working on briefs. I think I will call. Will you stick around?"

"Are you kidding? I wouldn't miss this for the world. But I would like that cup of coffee now."

"Oops! I forgot all about that. Sorry." I jumped up and headed for the kitchen.

"That's okay. I did too. Where do you keep the coffee? I can make some while you phone Jimmy-boy."

I turned and looked at Terri and laughed. "He'd die if you called him that to his face. He is definitely a James, not a Jimmy."

"I didn't realize it was so easy to commit murder." She leered at me.

"Stop it! You're giving me the creeps. What if someone murdered my mother? That thought has always preyed on my mind, somewhere back in the deep, dark recesses."

Terri leaned against the table while I rummaged

through my cupboards, searching for sugar packets for her coffee. She shook her head. "Great, and then you get mugged in the hospital parking lot. Got anything stronger than coffee?"

I glanced at her over my shoulder. "I have an espresso setting on my coffee machine."

"That's not what I meant. I meant stronger as in alcoholic."

"Oh. How stupid of me. I have some wine in the pantry. I shut the cupboard and gestured at the cabinet closest to the table. "Help yourself." I opened the next cupboard over and pulled out two wine glasses and handed them to Terri. "Here, pour me some too please." I grabbed the corkscrew from the drawer closest to the fridge.

With full wine glasses in hand, we returned to the living room. I rifled the drawer of my end table, looking for my address book. "Here it is," I said, picking up the book. I flipped it open to H and found "Higgins, James."

I clicked on the lamp, picked up the phone, and dialed his number. I paced back and forth in the living room, waiting for him to answer. After the third ring, his answering machine started. "You've reached the residence of James Higgins. I'm incapacitated at the moment. Please leave your name and number at the tone. Thank you." After a momentary pause, I heard the customary beep.

"James, it's Liz. If you're home, please pick up the phone. It's important."

"Hello? Liz?" I could barely hear my brother as he whispered into the phone.

"James? Did I wake you?"

"No, my voice is just a little hoarse right now. I think I'm coming down with something. Is Dad all right?"

"He's fine. That's not why I'm calling. I just needed to ask you a question."

"Don't they have lawyers in Florida?"

"Don't tease me, James. This is serious, and it's not a legal question. It's about Mother."

His tone took on a professional quality as he said, "What is it?"

"James, I know you have always been very closed-mouthed about what happened to Mother. I gave up a long time ago trying to get information out of you, but just once I'd like a straight answer from you."

"Fair enough. Fire away. I'll tell you anything I can."

"You will?" I asked stunned by his cooperative tone.

"Sure."

"Okay, well then, where is Mother?"

"I don't know."

"I thought you said you would tell me anything you could."

"I did, and I meant it, Liz. I don't know where she is now. I haven't heard from her in years."

"But you used to know where she was?"

"Yes."

"For the sake of my sanity, would you tell me everything you do know about Mother's disappearance?"

"All right. Are you ready?"

"Of course I'm ready. I wouldn't have called if I weren't."

"Mom left Dad because he had been seeing other women."

"What?!?!?" I shouted into the phone.

"I thought you said you were ready," he said

gently.

"I did, but that's not what I thought you were going to tell me."

"What did you think I was going to tell you?"

"Oh, I don't know. Something along the lines of Mother getting pregnant again. That she didn't want the baby, but that Dad did; so she ran away to get an abortion."

The laughter on the other end of the line filled me with embarrassment. "Where on earth did you get that idea?"

"I don't know. I just didn't know what to think."

"Do you now?"

"What do you mean?"

"Aren't you wondering why Mom didn't take you and Melissa?"

Fear and an overwhelming sense of rejection filled my eyes with tears. "Well, why didn't she?" I sat down in my chair and glanced up at Terri, who was now standing in the doorway between the kitchen and the living room.

"I don't know exactly. I guess she was so desperate to get away from Dad that she was prepared to do anything. She did not want Dad to find her. As it was, I had to talk to the police and explain the situation to them. Apparently they took my word for it, because they didn't expend much energy looking for her. But if she had taken you and Melissa, there would have been an extensive search and a court battle when they found her. I don't think she was capable of dealing with that at the time. She was wise enough to see that."

"You call abandoning your children wise?" I leaned forward and put my free hand over my forehead, closing my eyes tightly to stop the tears from coming.

"Liz, I know it must hurt like hell to hear this. That's why I kept it to myself all these years. I didn't want to tell you when you were still a kid. I thought that you would be better off thinking that she had been kidnapped or something. I figured you would get around to asking me again, sooner or later."

"Does Stan know?"

"Yes. I told him after a couple years passed. He was really pissed at Dad."

"Right now, I think I'm still too mad at Mother to consider how I feel about Dad." I said quietly.

"Well, try not to be too hard on either of them. Things don't take place in a vacuum. Mom did what she thought was best. I'm not sure she had any other options. Who did she have who would've helped her?"

"What about Grandma and Grandpa? They were still alive then."

"Yeah, and they would have slammed the door in her face. They didn't care much for Dad to begin with. They probably would have said, 'You made your bed; now lie in it.' They were very conservative and did not believe in divorce."

"Well, why didn't she just go to Nevada and get a divorce?"

"Liz, Mom didn't have any money of her own. Dad gave her money for the groceries every week. That's it. If she wanted clothes, she had to ask for them, and then he would go with her to buy them. She couldn't even go off shopping by herself."

"But Dad had plenty of money. Why didn't he let her have any of it?"

"I think he was afraid she would do exactly what she did. He probably figured that he'd be able to chain her to him if he could keep her 'barefoot and pregnant.' That saying had a whole of truth behind it. Besides, she would have still ended up having to fight him for custody of you and Melissa. Otherwise, what would be the point in divorcing him? I don't think she was interested in remarrying. She didn't want to finish back where she started."

"Shit! Now I hate his guts. Damn it, James! I wish I would have known all this crap before." I stood up and resumed my pacing.

"Why? So you could have spent your adolescent years angry?"

"What about Melissa?"

"What about her?"

"Shouldn't she be told?"

"Sure. When she's ready to hear it, she'll ask. You did, didn't you?"

"Yeah, but she was so young at the time. She hardly even remembers Mother."

"And you would like for me to tarnish her image of her only remaining parent?"

"Isn't the truth better than lies?"

"Who's lying to her, Liz? All I'm doing is waiting for her to ask."

"You'd tell her now even though she's still living with Dad?"

"Yes, I'd tell her now. I would've told you, had you asked when you were her age. I think she's old enough to know the truth. She'll know when she's ready to hear it. I have no doubt you'll see to that, now that you know."

"You mean you wouldn't mind if I told her?"

James sighed slowly and deeply. "Liz, I'd be delighted if you told her when she is ready to hear it. Do you think I have enjoyed holding the keys to the family closet all these years?"

"I guess not. I can't believe Dad was such a..."

"Bastard?" James offered, trying to be helpful.

"Jerk!"

"You know, Liz, Dad doesn't see things the way he used to. He went through hell when Mom left. He knew deep down that he was the reason you and Melissa were left motherless. I don't think he has ever forgiven himself for that. I think that is why he has always tried to give you two everything you wanted. He didn't want you two growing up spoiled, but neither did he want you to feel deprived. He's not all bad. You know that, I think."

"Yes, I know. I'm just really stunned by all this." I stopped pacing and put my hand on my forehead again, trying to protect it from the headache that was threatening to come back.

"Are you going to be all right?"

"What do you mean?"

"It's just that it is getting awfully late, and I have just given you a lot to think about. Do you have anyone you can talk with about these things?"

"As a matter of fact, I have a friend over now."

"Oh? Anyone I know?"

"I doubt it. She's a doctor at Lakeland Regional. She's been helping to look after Dad."

"Liz, don't tell me you're sleeping with one of Dad's doctors." He sounded impressed.

I sighed. "No James, not yet."

"Oh, well, good luck then. Call me again, if you need to. I'm always available for you."

"Thanks James, I might take you up on that. Good night."

Chapter Five

As soon as I hung up the phone, Terri walked into the living room with a glass of wine in her hand. "I tried not to listen, but your apartment isn't nearly big enough for me to get out of earshot. Drink your wine," she said, handing me the glass from the end table. She took a sip from her own glass. "I hope I didn't open a can of worms. It sounded as though your brother's revelation was more painful than intriguing."

"It was," I replied after a long sigh. I slumped down into the couch's comfortable upholstery and set my glass on the coffee table in front of me.

"If you want to tell me, I'm a good listener. If it's too painful or too private, then I understand."

The tears welled up in my eyes again. "I don't know what to think." At this point my inner dam burst wide open in a flood of painful tears.

In a split second Terri was by my side on the couch, wrapping her arms around me. She stroked my hair as she held me to her breast. "I'm sorry, Liz. I shouldn't have pushed you to call him. I should have realized that you'd had enough trauma for one day."

Through the racking sobs, I managed to say, " It's not your fault. You didn't know what James was going to tell me. I thought we had it all figured out. I never expected the answers I got."

Terri held me tighter. "Do you think you could take a sip of wine now? It might help calm your nerves." She reached over and picked up the glass I had set down on the coffee table.

I sat up a little and took a swallow. I felt the

warmth of the alcohol spread throughout my body. I began to calm down again. I returned the glass to the table and sat back against the couch cushions

"Thanks," I whispered. "I'm sorry I'm falling apart. I'm not usually like this."

"It's okay, Liz. Just relax. I don't expect anything in particular out of you. And I'm certainly not going to start making evaluations of your character on the basis of a hellish day like today."

Her words, and my sudden emotional outburst, made me realize that I had been more upset by the mugging than I had realized.

"Why would anyone want to attack me, Terri? I wasn't carrying a purse. I wasn't even dressed very well. Who would want to mug someone like me?"

"Oh god, Liz, I don't know. It's a crazy world sometimes. There are a lot of things I don't understand about it. Hell, it was probably just a matter of bad timing."

I sat up and took another sip of wine. I looked at Terri. Compassion was spilling over from her into my heart.

"Thanks for being here. Would you mind staying the rest of the night?"

"Of course I wouldn't mind. Do you want to talk, or do you need to go to bed? How can I help you?"

"I think I would like some music. Something soothing." I got up from the couch and walked over to the entertainment center. "I think some light jazz should help. Have you ever heard of David Benoit?"

"No, but I rarely listen to music. I never have time."

"That seems to be a recurring theme in your life."

"Tell me about it," Terri responded with a sardonic smile.

I started David Benoit's "Waiting for Spring" CD. On my way over to the couch, I turned off the lamp. "Do you mind the darkness? It helps me relax."

"I don't mind the darkness, if you don't mind me falling asleep on you again. If you want me to sit up in the dark with you, then I'll have to go make myself some coffee."

"Would you fall asleep if you were standing up?"

"No, probably not, but I don't want to stand up all night. What did you have in mind?"

"Would you like to dance with me? It wouldn't be tiring, as it would be little more than swaying to the music."

"Liz?"

"What?"

"You don't have to try to sell me on dancing with you. I'd love to sway to the music with you."

She got to her feet as she said this. I walked towards her, suddenly shy. It was all right though, because Terri wasn't a bit shy. She put her arms around me. "I'm taller, so I get to lead."

I giggled a Melissa-like giggle and relaxed into her embrace. It felt good to have her comforting arms wrapped around me. I was definitely in need of a woman's touch.

After a few moments of swaying to the light tune, Terri spoke up quietly. "Liz?"

"Yes?" I whispered.

"I'm glad you don't want to do anything more than sway to the music."

"Why is that?"

"Because I would never be able to dance to this music. It has no distinct beat."

"Some of the songs have a beat. The important thing is that you can just relax. You don't have to worry about trying to keep up with the beat."

"Liz?"

"Terri?"

"Do you like anything normal?"

"What's that supposed to mean?"

"You're just so different from anyone else I have ever met."

"Is that intended as a compliment or a put-down?"

"Neither. Just a statement of fact."

"Oh." I pondered this for a moment.

"Liz?" She whispered.

I lifted my head and looked at her, wondering what might be coming next.

"Would you slap me if I tried to kiss you?"

I smiled playfully. "Maybe, maybe not. You could always try it and see what happens." I tucked my head against her chest.

She laughed softly. "Yes, I suppose I could."

"Terri?"

"Yes, Liz?"

"Are you going to try it?" I lifted my head to look at her again.

She wrinkled her forehead as though she were giving it more consideration. "Maybe, maybe not. I'm still trying to decide whether it's worth the risk of getting slapped. I'm not very good at handling rejection."

I smiled again. "Terri?"

"Yes, Liz?" She relaxed into a sweet smile.

"I never slap women who try to kiss me."

"Oh, I see." She pulled me close to her again.

"No, you don't. It's too dark in here to see," I mumbled into her chest.

"This is true."

"Terri, when did you realize I was lesbian?"

Her chest rumbled with a stifled laugh. "When you opened the elevator door and stood there gawking at my backside."

"I was that obvious?"

Terri nodded slightly. "You were that obvious. But just to make sure I asked your little sister."

"You didn't!" I stepped back and squinted at her.

"I did." She smiled mischievously.

"What if she had been unaware of my orientation?"

"Ha! There is very little that escapes that young lady's notice." Terri pulled me back into her embrace.

"What do you mean?"

"Just what I said. Does she realize yet that she is lesbian?"

"Not enough to admit it."

"It's only a matter of time. Someone will come her way sooner or later."

I sighed. "I think she has a crush on you."

Terri paused in her swaying. "Really? I'm flattered."

"Perhaps you should save a place on your dance card for her."

"Perhaps. She's very cute." She resumed swaying.

"I know. She may be my nemesis yet."

"But she's awfully young. Is she even legal yet?"

"Yes, she's eighteen." I looked up at Terri again. "How old are you?"

"Twenty-seven. How about you?"

"Twenty-eight. Maybe I should lead since I'm older."

She shook her head. "Nope. It says in the official rule book for lesbians that the taller woman always leads."

"What rule book?"

"You know, the unwritten one." She winked at me.

"Then it must have been revised since the fifties. That one said that the butch was supposed to lead. It said nothing about height requirements." I snuggled against her chest again.

"It's quite apparent, Liz, that you haven't caught up with the times. All those strict rules about butch-femme roles were nixed a long time ago."

I nodded once. "I'm glad. It makes for a lot more freedom, though freedom can be pretty frightening sometimes."

"Tell me about it. Besides you're not very butch." She let her hand fall from my waist to the small of my back.

"No, I suppose not. Terri?"

"Yes, Liz?" She stroked my back lightly.

"Whatever happened to that kiss?" I lifted my face towards hers.

"It's still here waiting." She smiled ever so slightly.

"What is it waiting for?"

"The right moment," she whispered.

"Mm. And when will that be?"

"We'll know it when it arrives." She nodded slightly.

"Are you sure?

"Have I ever lied to you, Liz?" She raised her eyebrow inquisitively at me.

"How am I supposed to know that? I just met you, um, twenty-one hours ago."

"Is that all? And you're impatient for a kiss already? You sure move fast." She smiled deeply, her teeth gleaming in the dark.

"Hey, it was your idea." I smacked her lightly on the arm.

"Phooey. It wasn't only my idea. I just asked first. You're the one who asked me to dance." She tried to pull me back to her chest, but I pulled back. She stopped dancing and looked at me. "You can't say that you had not already thought about kissing me, can you?"

I smiled. "No, I can't. But I bet you thought about kissing me long before you asked me."

She started dancing again and pulled me back to her chest. "Maybe, maybe not."

"You're teasing me." I whacked her on the arm again.

"Yep! Guilty as charged." She squeezed me gently. "Terri?" .

Terri took a long, deep breath "Yes Liz?"

"Is it the right time yet?" I looked up at her.

She leaned down towards me. "What do you think?"

"It depends."

She pulled back again. "On what?"

"On whether or not you will be thinking about Melissa when you kiss me."

She stopped dancing again and tilted her head to the side in puzzlement. "Liz?"

"Yes, Terri?"

"Why do you always sell yourself short?"

"I don't." I frowned at her.

"Yes you do, quite frequently."

"I thought you weren't going to make any evaluations about my character based on one hellish day."

She nodded at me. "This is true. I did say that. I'm sorry. Perhaps I should have said, 'Do you always sell yourself short? Or is it just that you have had a rough day?'" She pulled me back into a light embrace.

"That would have been more fair, and I don't know whether I always sell myself short. I don't think I do. Then again, when it comes to my sister, I think I usually do."

"Why is that?" She stroked my lower back again.

"Probably just because she has homecoming queen looks, a flawless body, and a sweet personality to go with it."

"True. But other than that, what does she have?"

I laughed. "A good head on her shoulders and a lesbian perspective on life."

"Well, that clenches it." She stopped dancing and put her hands on her hips.

"Clenches what?" I asked, a little startled.

"I've decided to ask your little sister for a date."

"Are you teasing me again?"

"Yes, I am." She put her hands back on my waist and started swaying as the next song began to play. "Liz, how do you think your sister describes you?"

"I don't know."

"Would you mind it if I asked her some time?"

"I suppose not."

"I'm sorry you feel as though you are not as good as your sister. I think you are very interesting."

"Thank you, Terri, but interesting is not quite the same thing as beautiful, shapely, sweet, and smart."

"Liz?"

"Yes, Terri?" I looked up at her.

"I think you are all those things," she said softly.

"Really?" I whispered.

"Really," she whispered back.

"Terri?"

"Yes Liz, it's time." She leaned towards me and her lips parted.

Chapter Six

Just before our lips met, the doorbell rang. "Damn!" I said, as Terri and I quickly released each other and stepped back.

"Who could that be?" Terri asked clearly agitated.

I switched the lamp on. "Ten-to-one, it's Melissa. No one else shows up at my door at one o'clock on a Saturday morning." I walked over to the door, spied through the peek hole, and unbolted the door, admitting one smiling teenager.

"Hi, Liz. I didn't wake you, did I? I know you're usually up at this time, but I wasn't sure, since . . . oh, Dr. Jackson! I didn't realize you were still here. Oh god, I'm not interrupting anything, am I? Of course, I am. What am I saying? How stupid of me. See you later, Liz."

Melissa said all of this with barely a pause in between sentences. As she spun around to beat a hasty retreat, I grabbed her by the shirtsleeve. "It's okay, Melissa, you can come in. Did you just get off work?"

"Yeah, it was another exciting Friday night at the pizza parlor."

"You work at a pizza parlor?" Terri's eyebrows rose in unison at this revelation.

"Yep, and I have a pizza in the car if you're interested in sharing it with me. I didn't bring it in with me, because I wasn't sure if Liz was going to be up to having company. I knew she wouldn't eat any of it, but she doesn't usually mind it if I scarf some down after work. I'm always starved when I work this late."

"I can imagine," Terri sympathized. "I think I'd be

starved just from working around pizza all night. What kind is it?"

After a quick glance at Liz, Melissa said, "Pepperoni and mushrooms. What do you say?"

"Sounds great! I'm hungry again anyway. I never eat much when I'm at the hospital, but I always manage to catch up on my days off."

"Well," I said, "it seems we're in for a pizza party. Go get your pizza, Melissa. If it needs to be reheated, my oven is yours," I offered magnanimously. To Terri, I said, "Well, it looks like you get to have pizza after all."

"Do you mind?"

"Of course not. I'm glad Melissa came back. I had no idea you had gotten hungry again."

"I didn't either until she mentioned pizza. Then my stomach alarm went off with a fury. It does that sometimes."

Melissa banged her elbow against the door to announce her return. I opened the door for her. She glided in, bearing two large pizza boxes. "There are actually two different kinds. The other one has black olives and onions."

Terri looked pleased. "Sounds delicious. I like just about anything on pizza, except anchovies. They're a little too salty for me."

"Me too," was Melissa's response.

"I'll put on some more music while you two decide whether your pizza needs to be heated."

"Could you just turn on the radio, Liz? I'm too wired to listen to your jazz muzak stuff."

I smiled politely. "Sure, Melissa. What station?"

"99.9, of course."

Terri interjected, "That's the one I listen to in my car."

"I thought you didn't listen to the radio much," I said, a little annoyed.

"I don't much. I'm usually at the hospital, not in my car."

"Of course," I said, switching the stereo to the FM radio mode. I let the tuner search for the requested station. As usual, it landed on an even digit. "I hope 99.8 is close enough. This digital tuner can only count by two's."

"Oh I know, your car stereo does that too."

Great, I thought, *I'll have to change both radios back to my station.*

I was feeling petty, and I knew it. I don't know what it is about Melissa. I know she doesn't try to make me feel like a social outcast, but that's how I feel sometimes when I'm with her. It gets worse if anyone else is around. Suddenly I become Melissa's quaint yet slightly eccentric sister.

A roar of laughter escaped from the kitchen. "Well, it sounds like those two have hit it off," I mumbled to myself.

Suddenly, Melissa appeared in the kitchen doorway. "Liz, do you want anything at the 7-11? I'm going to run out and get some cokes."

"No thanks. Do you still have the keys?"

"No, I laid them on the table, but Terri gave me her keys. She said that I could take her car."

"Fine. See you later."

Melissa bounded through the living room and out the front door. I walked into the kitchen to find Terri seated at the table deep in thought. "A penny for your thoughts."

"Don't waste your money. I was just thinking about a patient. Sometimes it's hard to shut my medical mind off after hours."

"I see. I thought maybe you were thinking about how to tell me that you like my sister better than me."

Terri looked up at me. "Liz, am I doing something wrong? You keep setting me up as the bad guy. Do you want me to go after your sister, or are you just daring me to choose you over her? Is there something about me in particular that you distrust, or am I just walking into the middle of an ongoing sibling rivalry?"

I sat down in the chair opposite Terri and stared down at my feet. "I don't know. I never really considered Melissa as a threat before. She has always had a boyfriend, so until recently I had assumed that she was heterosexual. But the older she gets the more I wonder. Then after watching her today, I realized that she's behaving in the same flirtatious manner with you that she uses with her boyfriends. I guess I'm just feeling really insecure. I'm afraid I'll lose my new friend before I get a chance to know her." I looked up at Terri and found only kindness in her eyes.

"Okay. Let's say I do fall for your little sister, and she falls for me. How would you feel about that?"

"I think I would feel cheated and jealous."

"Because you lost me, or because it was your sister who got me?"

"I'm not sure."

"Okay, let's say I fall in love with someone else—a neighbor, let's say. How would you feel?"

"Mm. Not the same. I would be hurt, but not devastated since we only just met."

"So this probably has more to do with your sister than it does me."

"Sounds like it."

"Then please don't make me out to be the bad guy. I like your sister. She's cute. A little young, but definitely attractive. I don't know if I'm ever going to feel anything beyond that. For all we know, she may not come to realize and accept her orientation for another ten years. I'm not planning on waiting around until then. I have a life to live. A career to pursue."

"And what do you think about me?"

"Essentially the same thing. I find you attractive and interesting. You're closer to my age, so that's not an issue. Beyond that, I don't know yet. I do know that I don't want to get in the middle of a sibling battle. I'm not a prize for the best sister to win. If you would like to start seeing each other, I'm interested. If you want to use me to prove something to your sister, then I'm not."

Just then Melissa came back. She came into the kitchen breathless, arms full of cokes and chips. She took one look at my face. "Why do I get the feeling that I'm interrupting again?"

I sighed. "It's all right, Melissa. I'm just being weird as usual. I think I might just go to bed. You two can sleep over, if you want to. I assume Dad won't care since he's not home anyway. Enjoy yourselves. There are plenty of blankets in the linen closet. I'll get another pillow."

I dug up another pillow and blanket for Melissa to use. Stacking them on the couch, I said, "Good night. I apologize for being such a wet blanket. I think this day has done more damage than I thought."

"Good night, Liz," said Melissa, with concern in her voice.

"Good night, Liz," said Terri sadly.

As I walked back to my bedroom, I heard Melissa

say, "I really did interrupt something, didn't I? I'm really sorry. I came back here because I didn't want to stay at the house alone again. It's too quiet with no one else there. Besides, I was worried about Liz. She took a pretty good bump on the head."

I laughed when I heard this last remark. Then I sighed and wondered whether it would be realistic to blame all of this on one little bump. Somehow I didn't think so. It was true enough that I'd had a trying day. Between being mugged and finding out that my mother abandoned me because my father was unfaithful, it was all just a little bit too much. Perhaps I was being a little bit crazy when it came to Melissa and Terri. And even if they did end up together, I should be happy for them.

Back in my bedroom, I felt rather isolated. Still it felt better to be in bed than it did to be out there trying to fit in where I didn't belong. *I suppose I am a little eccentric. I don't try to be different; I don't try to be anything, really, except myself.* With these thoughts floating around in my head, I fell into a blissful state of sleep.

Chapter Seven

I awoke that morning around eleven, feeling rested and refreshed. Only the bump on the back of my head remained to remind me of my experience in the hospital parking lot. *If it weren't for this knot on my head, I would think that yesterday was nothing more than a nightmare. Unfortunately though, yesterday did happen and today, Liz, you have to live with the consequences.*

I strolled out to the living room expecting to find two sleeping women. Instead I found only Melissa. I sat down in my rocking chair and stared at Melissa's sleeping form. This time I resisted the temptation to draw a picture, mostly because my sister's face was covered partially by a blanket.

My presence must have penetrated her sleep-laden consciousness, because she suddenly stirred in her sleep. "Liz?"

"Yes, Melissa?"

"What time is it?"

"It's almost eleven o'clock. When did Terri go home?"

"Around two-thirty, I think. Did we keep you awake?"

"No, not at all. I think I crashed pretty quickly."

"How's your head?"

"Still there, I presume. It doesn't hurt much anyway."

"Good."

"Melissa, what was the first thing you thought of when you woke up just now?"

"Am I awake? Darn, I thought I was dreaming. Well, the first thing I thought about when I woke up was the same thing I think of every morning when I wake up."

"And that is?"

"Where's the bathroom? I really need to go."

"Are you serious?"

"Very," she said, sitting up quickly. Then she rushed off to the bathroom. When she came back she looked much more awake, but still a little puzzled. She sat down on the couch and ran her hand through her long blonde hair in attempt to bring it under control. It didn't work. Several strands fell right back down in her face. She slumped back against the pillow. "So, why did you want to know what I thought of first thing this morning?"

"Just curious. What did you think of after you thought about the bathroom?"

"I wondered what time it was, remember?"

"Why did you want to know what time it was?"

"Because I wanted to know whether I should get up or go back to sleep. I'm supposed to go to movies with Robert this afternoon. I didn't want to sleep too long, since I want to visit Dad first."

"Oh. Do you feel like you have a good relationship with Dad?"

"I guess so. Why do you ask?"

"Just curious."

"Liz, are you okay?"

"Yes. Why?"

"Because you're being weird this morning."

"I thought you were of the opinion that I am always weird."

She looked startled. "Where did you get that idea?"

"That's the way you always treat me, like I'm eccentric."

She grimaced and shook her head. "No, I don't. I think you're different, but you say that all the time, and I think you're right. You eat differently; you listen to different music; you see the world differently. Liz, you don't even own a television set."

"So?"

"So, in this country most people do."

"I don't like television."

"I know. That's just it. You like very few things most people in our culture like. That makes you different. I never said that it made you weird. I just figured it was part of your artistic temperament or whatever. I like you, Liz. I have a lot of respect for you."

"You're serious, aren't you?"

"Of course, I'm serious. What's eating at you? Does this have anything to do with Terri?"

"Why do you say that?"

"She asked me last night what I thought about you. Now this morning you're asking me all these crazy questions. What's going on?"

"What did you tell Terri?"

"I told her what I just told you. I have a lot of respect for you because you're not afraid to be different. You're true to yourself. Most people aren't. They do what people think they should do."

"Is that what you do?"

"Sometimes. It's hard not to in high school. You don't have many options there."

"What kind of options would you like to have?"

She sighed. "I don't know. I look at your life, and I see how you chose to do what you loved to do, instead of working somewhere that could provide better job security and more money. I see how successful you've become doing what you love. I know it hasn't always been easy for you. I remember what it was like when you first started. You would get worried that you weren't going to make enough money to pay your rent.

"Dad used to tell me that he wished he could help you out financially, but he knew you wanted to make it on your own. So he didn't pressure you to take money, even when he knew you could use it. He has also told me a million times how proud he is of you."

"Yeah, he's told me that too. I guess I had just forgotten that part of him."

She looked at me with concern in her eyes. "What's the matter, Liz?"

I pulled my feet up into the chair and hugged my knees to my chest. "Oh, I just had a disturbing conversation with James last night."

"What about?"

"Dad and Mother."

She looked puzzled. "What did James say that was so disturbing?"

"I don't know if you want to know."

"It can't be much worse than what Dad has told me."

Feeling suddenly defensive about my mother, I said, "What has Dad told you?"

"He told me that he was the reason why Mother left us."

"And?"

"He said that he had been foolish when he was younger. He had taken lovers after he married, mostly because he was trying to make Mother jealous. He also said that he had not treated her very kindly. He never allowed her to have any money of her own because he was afraid she would use it to leave him."

"That's what James told me too. How long have you known all this?"

"Dad told me a couple years ago, I guess. I started asking him a lot of questions about Mother."

"I'm surprised he told you all that. He never told me anything."

"Did you ask him?"

"No. I didn't think he knew what happened to Mother."

"He didn't exactly. She was never found, and he never heard from her again. But he's sure she left him, and he knows it was his fault."

Tears started running down my cheeks. "I can't believe you knew all this stuff and I didn't."

Melissa leaned towards me and put a hand on my knee. "Liz, if I had known that you didn't know, I would have told you. I'm sorry. I just assumed that you knew because you were so much older than I was when she left."

"James thought I was too young at the time to be told the whole story. If I hadn't finally asked him again last night, I don't think he would have ever told me."

"Is that what has been making you ask crazy questions this morning?"

"Yes and no. It's part of it."

"Would you care to confide in me with the rest of it?" Melissa settled back on the couch.

"Well, it all started with meeting Terri. I was attracted to her as soon as I laid eyes on her. After we had coffee yesterday morning, I knew that I wanted to get to know her better, but I also knew that we were radically different. Then after watching you interact with her, I realized that you and she would make a better couple than she would and I would."

Melissa giggled. "Liz, you seem to keep forgetting that I have a boyfriend."

"No I haven't. What were you telling me a little while ago about wishing you had more options in high school? You never did explain what options you would like. I suspect that one of those options has to do with dating. Am I right?"

"All right, Liz, I admit it. I have thought about what it would be like to be in a lesbian relationship. The only problem is that girls never ask me out and guys do. I go places with my female friends, but I'm not attracted to any of them."

"What about Terri?"

She shrugged dismissively. "Well, I'm definitely drawn to her. Unfortunately I don't know what to do about it. To begin with, she's a lot older than I am. I can't imagine what we would have to talk about, other than the stupid things I talk to my other girlfriends about."

"Which is?"

"Rock bands, football games, boyfriends. Somehow, I don't think that would hold Terri's interest long. My word, Liz, she's a doctor. What do I have in common with her? I already found out that she doesn't run. According to her, she gets enough exercise running from emergency to emergency."

"I guess I hadn't thought about all that."

"Look, Liz, I don't know whether you two would be good for each other or not, but I don't see the point in missing your chance to find out. She may not be around much longer."

"I think that may be part of the problem too. I don't want to fall for her just to have her move to another state. Long distance relationships don't work for me." I laid my head on my knees and closed my eyes momentarily.

"Aha! I think I just got the connection. Are you afraid you'll fall in love with Terri, then she'll abandon you like Mother did?"

I lifted my head and looked at my sister. "Where did you get that little insight?"

"I don't know. Am I right?"

"I don't know either, but it's worth thinking about. It sounds all too plausible in light of the recent emotional upheaval."

"Well, do you mind if I let you think about it while I drive us over to see Dad?"

"Mm. That's fine."

We both dressed quickly and got into the car. It felt strange to be in the passenger's seat of my own car. I must've been too wiped out to notice it the day before. As we drove across town to the hospital, I started thinking about our conversation again.

"Melissa, do you think you'll ever find out for yourself what it's like to be lesbian?"

"I don't know. For you, it's all so easy. I'm not you. It may come as a surprise to you, but I would like to have kids some day."

"Really? I didn't know that. But there are lesbians who have children, you know."

"No, actually, I didn't know that. How on earth do they manage that?"

"Physically or financially?"

"Both, I guess."

"Some find a willing sperm donor. Some adopt, though that's kind of tricky because of attitudes and laws about same-sex couples raising children. For lots of women, however, the realization that they are lesbian doesn't come until after they get married and have children. They may get dissatisfied with their marriage, or they may meet a woman who turns their world upside down. Any number of things can happen.

"Frankly I think that a lot of women are more lesbian than they think. Their biological desire to have children leads them to think that they need a man too. When their biological need to bear children is met, they wake up one morning, look at the guy lying next to them, and wonder who the hell he is and how he got there."

"How do you know all that?"

"Well, for one thing I try to stay current on issues that affect the gay community by reading lesbian and gay publications. There's a lot of controversy about our right to parent. Some gays and lesbians are trying to gain custody of their kids from a previous marriage. Some are attempting to adopt someone else's unwanted children. There have also been some legal problems that have arisen with lesbians who have been artificially inseminated. Sperm donors who were originally not interested in parenting the resulting offspring change their mind and sue for visitation rights."

"We've made some inroads in this area, but there are still too many homophobes running our government and presiding over our courts. They seem to think that homosexuality is a valid reason to deny us the right to raise children. It's pretty outrageous when you think about it. But I have hope that things will change eventually. They've already changed a lot since the seventies.

"Think about the choices you would have, Melissa, if our society didn't make such a big deal about homosexuality. If people didn't fight over whether gay parents should have custody of their children or have the right to adopt other people's children."

Melissa looked thoughtful for a moment then said slowly. "Things would certainly be different."

"They sure would. But let's talk specifically about the difference it could make in your life. Are you interested in Robert because he might make a good father one day, or because he's the person who can help you become all that you're meant to be?"

"God, I don't know. Right now I'm just trying to finish high school in good standing. Then hopefully I can get a track scholarship for college so I can run and learn at the same time. I don't want to get married and have kids right away."

"But do you really want to get married at all? Or do you just want to have children?"

"Well, I sure don't want to have to raise them by myself, if that's what you mean."

"I understand your wanting a co-parent, but there are lesbians who want to co-parent too. No matter what the religious right and the conservative courts might say, parenting is not an exclusively heterosexual thing."

"I never thought about it that way, I guess. I just grew up thinking that a girl grows up, falls in love with a man, gets married, has babies, has a job or career maybe."

"That's what we are all taught to think pretty much."

"But that's not what you're doing with your life. Are you happy? Do you want children?"

"Yes, I am happy. No, I don't want children. My artistic creations are my babies. I give birth to visual concepts. I put my imprint on the world through my art. I don't think I would make a good parent because of all the energy that goes into my creative efforts."

"But you can't cuddle a painting."

I laughed. "No, you can't cuddle a painting. I never thought of it that way. But occasionally I do get to cuddle a lover. That goes a long way for me."

"Maybe you should get a dog or cat."

I shook my head. "I don't think so. This apartment complex is pretty strict about that. And besides, an animal might get into my art supplies and make a mess."

"I don't know how you can stand to live by yourself. One night alone was enough for me. I thought it would be so cool to stay by myself while Dad was in the hospital, but it wasn't. I got scared and could hardly sleep. By seven o'clock, I had decided to run back down to the hospital to see you and Dad before I went to school.

"That's how I found out you were in the emergency room, by the way. Nobody knew who you were because you didn't have any identification on you. You were just lying on that bed in the emergency room, passed out cold. I only just happened to go in the wrong entrance because I got kind of turned around in the parking lot. I couldn't remember where I was supposed to park because I had parked Dad's car in the patients' parking lot the day before, while I was admitting him.

"As I was walking by, I just happened to glance into the room where you were and saw you lying there. I freaked, let me tell you. I thought for a moment that you were dead. I asked the nurse in your room what had happened to you. She told me what she knew then went off with the news that their mystery patient had been identified. She came back with a hospital band for your wrist and papers for me to sign. That's when I told them they needed to talk to Dad upstairs. I probably shouldn't have told them that, since they went up and told him about your situation. It probably made him worry unnecessarily. I just kind of lost it though and didn't know what to do." She gripped the steering wheel tightly enough to turn her knuckles white.

I reached over and squeezed her arm. "You did fine, Melissa. After all, what if I had been seriously injured? Dad needed to know at least. You did what you should have done."

"That's a relief. I've been wondering if I made Dad sicker because of telling him about you." She released her death grip on my car.

"Not to worry. Dad's stronger than he lets on, I think. I'm beginning to see that myself."

The conversation came to an abrupt halt as we pulled into the parking lot of the hospital. I shivered as I thought about what had happened here yesterday. My head responded with a pounding ache that lasted several seconds. I closed my eyes to let a wave of nausea roll over me.

Melissa leaned over to look at me more closely. "Are you okay, Liz? You don't look so good."

I opened my eyes and nodded my head weakly. "I think so. I'm afraid my body remembers yesterday better than I do. It seems to respond with pain whenever it encounters a reminder of my mugging experience."

"Maybe you should have Dr. Jackson check you out."

"Now that sounds like the best idea I've heard in a long time, but perhaps I should leave that up to her."

"Oh, Liz! I didn't mean it that way!"

I smiled at my remembrance of Terri's uplifted eyebrow. Then I sighed. "I hope Terri and I can somehow get on better footing. So far, we haven't done too well communicating with one another. Maybe we are both trying too hard. It was so easy to talk to her in the coffee shop that morning. I don't know what it is about the woman. She just seems to push all the wrong buttons in me. But at the same time, she's pushing all the right buttons. Maybe it's me. Maybe I'm the one who's pushing all the wrong buttons in me. She really hasn't done or said anything to offend me, yet I keep getting offended.

"Maybe I am eccentric. I thought I was just being individualistic. Perhaps I'm just a bitch after all. Now that's a sobering thought. But if I am a bitch, then I'm a bitch who can change, and I can start today by not bitching about being a bitch."

Melissa patted my leg gently. "Liz, calm down. You're not a bitch. And you're not eccentric. You just need to cut yourself some slack. My god, Liz, you were knocked over the head yesterday and robbed. Perhaps you're in shock. That was pretty traumatic. On top of that, you found out some things about Dad and Mother that you didn't know. That's all very hard."

I threw my head back against the headrest. "You're right, Melissa. I didn't mean to flake out on you. I guess I should go back home and go to bed. But I do need to visit Dad ever so briefly then run by the DMV to see if I can get a new driver's license. Everything else can wait for now."

I took a deep breath and mustered up the courage to face my father again, burdened with my new perspective of him. Overnight he had become the cheating man who drove his penniless wife into the world alone, definitely not a pretty picture to have of your own father. But from what Melissa had told me this morning, he had also paid a heavy price for having to face the truth about himself. It wouldn't be right for me to make him going on paying for his mistakes.

Chapter Eight

After a short visit with my father and a side trip to replace my driver's license, Melissa and I went to my apartment and ate lunch together. Our conversation was much more casual, though it was obvious that we were both still pondering our earlier conversations. It was a thoughtful Melissa who went off to the movies when her boyfriend came to get her.

As she was closing the door behind her, Melissa said, "Do you mind if I stay here one more night? I really hate staying at the house by myself."

"You're welcome any time, Melissa. You know that."

"Thanks," she said with a smile as the door closed.

I looked out the front window of my apartment and watched as Melissa and Robert walked to his car. I laughed to myself as I witnessed Robert's attempt to hold Melissa's hand and her subtle maneuverings that made it impossible for him to do so. How well I remembered those sudden urges to dig in my pocket for some nonexistent object just so I could avoid physical contact with my date. I was glad that I no longer had to pretend I enjoyed male advances. Feeling sorry for Melissa, I secretly vowed to help her find a lesbian friend.

About the time the young couple drove away, the phone rang. My heart skipped a beat. "I wonder if that's Terri." The phone rang again. "What if it is her? What will I say?" A third ring. "Oh shit, Liz, just answer the phone!"

Holding my breath, I picked up the receiver. "Hello?"

No response.

"Hello?" I said again, wondering if it was a bad connection, a computer call, or a just a wrong number. Just as I was getting ready to hang up, a male voice said, "Elizabeth Higgins?"

Not recognizing the voice, I said, "This is she. Who is this?"

"I'm the man who robbed you yesterday."

"What?"

"I'm the man who grabbed you yesterday in the hospital parking lot. I got your name and address off your drivers license."

I thought about hanging up, but figured I'd better find out what this guy wanted, so I could at least give the police a full report. "Look, I don't know what you want, so why don't you just leave me alone?"

"Of course you don't know what I want. How could you? I just wanted to know if you are the same Elizabeth Higgins who is an artist."

"Look, buddy, I don't give out information to people who refuse to identify themselves, so drop dead."

I hung up the phone and dialed the police. I told them about the phone call and the mugging incident. The woman I talked to urged me to come in and fill out a report on the mugging incident. In the meantime she would arrange for me to talk with someone about the phone call. As soon as I hung up the phone, it rang again.

"Oh, great. If that is Terri and I don't answer it, I will miss her call. On the other hand, if it is that nut, I don't want to answer it. This is when I need to have an answering machine."

I let it ring a couple more times then picked it up.

"Hello?"

"Hello, Liz? This is Terri."

I sighed audibly then said, "Thank goodness it's you."

"Liz, are you all right?"

"No, not really." I told her what had happened and how I had been afraid to answer the phone.

"Do you want me to go with you to the police station?"

"You can if you want to, though I hardly think that would be a fun way to spend your day off."

"It beats sitting around wondering what's going on."

"Okay, sure. I could probably use the emotional support."

"I'll be there in fifteen minutes."

"Great. See you then. Bye."

As I hung up the phone, I realized I was trembling. I decided to pour myself a glass of wine to see if it would calm my nerves. I figured Terri could drive to the station. On my way to kitchen, the phone rang again. Not thinking, I picked it up immediately.

As soon as I said "hello," I realized what I had done.

The male voice on the line said, "Well, you've been busy calling people since I talked to you last.

I hung up and walked into the kitchen. I decided to brew some soothing tea instead. That would require more physical movement than pouring a glass of wine.

The phone rang again.

I said to myself, "Now that shouldn't be Terri, since she's on her way over, so it's probably that nut. I'll just let it ring."

After a dozen rings, it finally stopped. Just as the teakettle began to whistle, there was a knock at the door.

"Oh shit," I said, as I grabbed the teakettle off the burner and went to open the door.

I looked through the peephole and saw Terri's face. As I opened the door, I said, with a flourish of the steaming kettle in my hand, "Come in, would you like some tea?"

"Tea? I thought we were on our way to the police station."

The phone rang. "Oh, no. That must be him again."

"How many times has he called since I talked to you?"

"Once that I know of. I quit answering it after that. Of course, I don't know if that is him or not. That's the frustrating thing. It could be someone else, someone I want to talk to."

"Let me answer it."

Just as I was about to say, "No, I don't think that would be a good idea," Terri picked up the receiver and said, "Hello?"

In spite of myself, I nearly laughed aloud. She had spoken in a very deep voice, one that didn't quite sound natural. In fact, it sounded exactly like a woman trying to sound like a man.

Suddenly, Terri said, "Well, screw you!" and slammed the phone down.

"What did he say?

"He said, 'Come on now, Elizabeth, I know you wouldn't have a man in your apartment. I know you're queer, though you won't be when I get finished with you.'"

"And that's when you said, 'Well, screw you?'"

"I guess that wasn't exactly the best thing to say. I'm sorry, Liz."

The sheepish look on her face made me laugh. In fact, the whole situation began to seem like a huge farce. "So, what this nutcase wants is to convert me to heterosexuality?"

"Apparently."

I walked back into the kitchen and set the tea kettle on a cool burner. Then I rejoined Terri in the living room. "You know, Terri, if this weren't so aggravating, I think I would find this whole scene very funny. At least I know what he's after now. That will help me with the police report. Let's hurry up and leave before he calls again."

"What about your tea?"

"Forget it. I want to get out of here before the phone rings again."

I locked the door and followed Terri's tall form outside. "I'm glad you're coming with me. I think I'd like for you to drive, if you don't mind."

"That's fine. We can take my car, if you'd like."

I nodded my head and followed her over to an old green Pontiac Catalina. Terri opened the door for me. "I'm not trying to be gallant. It's just that if you don't open it just right, it won't close again.

"I see. Does that mean that I have to wait for you to let me out too?"

"Unless you want to slide out the driver's side."

"That's sounds more like me. I never could stand to have men open car doors for me. I always felt as though it were somehow symbolic of the way our society works. You know, women will never get anywhere if men don't open the doors for them."

"Hmm. I never thought of it that way. I guess I always viewed it as a quaint custom. Something more along the lines of a servant opening doors for royalty."

"Even that leads to inequality between the sexes, since it makes men subservient to women."

"What's wrong with that?" She said with a gleam in her eye.

"Having men subservient to women is not only unlikely, it is dangerous. The lower class will always eventually rebel and seek to oppress its oppressors."

"I think we are talking about two different things. I'm not talking about communism and the huddled masses. I was just talking about antiquated, chivalrous customs."

"You're right, Terri. We are talking about two different things. Either that or we are talking about the same thing on two different wavelengths."

"I keep getting the feeling that you take things a lot more seriously than I do.

"Maybe I just take different things seriously."

"Yeah, I guess. Whatever. So, is this the right police station?" She pulled into the parking lot of the Lakeland Police Department.

"It's the only police station."

"Well, I haven't been around here very long."

"Right, and you don't get very far from the hospital either."

Terri put the car in park and looked at me intently. "Was that supposed to be sympathetic or sarcastic?"

I winced. "I was trying to be sympathetic, I think."

"You don't know for sure?"

"Well, I can't say that I care much for professions that leave its employees with little time to be human."

Terri shook her head slowly. "I am human, Liz. I really don't understand you sometimes. I keep getting the feeling that you don't approve of me for some reason."

"I'm sorry. I think it is just that we are so different."

"What's wrong with that? Isn't variety the spice of life?"

"So it's said, yet I know from experience that you can get an overdose of spices."

"So what you're saying is that we are too different."

I shrugged. "I don't know. Maybe."

She smiled slightly. "Maybe not."

I laughed at her allusion to our intimate conversation the previous night. "I supposed we had better go in. I guess you're a key witness to this stupid affair, so you may need to answer some questions too."

Terri opened the door, slid out from behind the steering wheel, and stood by the car, waiting for me to exit. I evacuated via the driver's side, shutting the door behind me.

"Do you need to lock it?"

Terri laughed out loud. "Anybody who is stupid enough to steal an old car that is parked in front of the police station deserves to be straddled with its idiosyncrasies."

I looked at Terri for a moment, enjoying her light-hearted perspective. Then I said in a serious tone, "Terri, I want to get to know you better, but I think I'm afraid to."

"Why?"

"For starters I'm afraid that our different perspectives and habits will make things very uncomfortable. I'm also afraid that you will have to move on just as we're beginning to get somewhere."

"Liz?"

"Yes, Terri?"

"I'm afraid of those things too."

"What do you think we should do about it?"

"Why don't we have dinner tonight and discuss it? You can pick the place since your diet is stricter than mine. I can eat nearly anything."

"How about my place?"

"You don't mind cooking?"

"No I really don't, and you don't even have to help."

"How about if I bring some wine or something?"

"Bring whatever you like."

Terri smiled. "It's a date. Now perhaps we should go in before we get arrested for loitering on government property."

"Mm. Good idea."

Chapter Nine

By the time we finished talking with the police detective about the mugging and the phone calls, it was nearly six o'clock. Terri drove me back to my apartment and dropped me off. "I'll be back within thirty minutes."

"Okay. See you."

I walked into my apartment, looking around to make sure everything was as it should be. Then I stripped off all my clothes, got into the shower, and racked my brain trying to think of something to fix for supper. The phone rang while I was in the shower, but I didn't get out to answer it. The police detective recommended that I avoid answering the phone for the next few days. He suggested that I set up a code with my close friends and family members, so they could get in contact with me.

As I got out of the shower, I heard the front door open. I froze. "Oh, shit. Now what am I going to do?" I locked the bathroom door then got dressed as quickly and quietly as I could. The phone rang again, and I heard Melissa's voice say, "Hello?"

Thank goodness, it's just Melissa.

Then I heard her say, "I don't know who you are, but you are really very childish and stupid, and I'm going to call the police, so they can trace this call."

I heard the phone slam down then Melissa called out, "Liz? Are you home?"

I came out of the bathroom so abruptly that I made Melissa jump. "Jeez, Liz, you scared the hell out of me! I just got a crank call."

"I know. I'm sorry you had to hear that. What did he say this time?"

"This time? How many times has he called?"

"Several. He claims to be the guy who mugged me in the parking lot."

"You're kidding!"

"No, I'm not. He must have he gotten my name and address off my driver's license. I assume he just looked me up in the directory and decided to give me a call. The weird thing is that he seems to know about my work. He asked me if I was Elizabeth Higgins the artist. Then Terri answered the phone once this afternoon when he called. He told her that he knew that I was queer and that he was going to change that personally. At least, that's the idea he conveyed, if not the exact words."

Melissa wrinkled her face in disgust. "Ew, gross! What a creep! Have you called the police?"

"Of course."

"What did they tell you to do?"

"They suggested that I not answer the phone for a few days."

Melissa shook her head. "Gee, Liz, I could have told you that much. They didn't offer you protection or anything?"

"They did say that they would patrol the area more frequently for the next couple of days."

"That's something anyway. Jeez, Liz, what if he cuts the phone lines and breaks in?"

"Please, Melissa, I'm not living in the back woods somewhere. There are people in the apartments on both sides of me. I can always scream for help. The walls are thin enough to hear anything above conversation level."

"That's true, and I'll be here tonight. Maybe we can get Terri to stay all night too. On second thought, if Terri comes over, then maybe I should leave."

I smiled at her, "No, Melissa, please stay. Perhaps if you're around, we won't get into any more stupid discussions. You can always kick me under the table if I start getting too weird."

"My pleasure," she retorted, grinning mischievously.

"Right now though I need to figure out what I'm going to fix for supper."

"Why don't you make Mexican food? Most people like that."

"Hmm, that's one possibility. I think I have some cooked beans in the freezer. I'll have to thaw them in the microwave though, but that shouldn't take too long. What about nachos?"

"Sounds good to me. I can chop up veggies to put on top."

"Perfect. You're sweet, Melissa." I leaned over and kissed her on the cheek.

She smiled warmly at me. "Of course I am."

"You can turn on the radio, if you'd like," I offered, trying to be more tolerant of other people's music tastes.

"Only if we put it on your station. I've listened to enough rock for one day. The movie Robert and I went to see was about a rock star. It was positively deafening. Right now I would prefer to listen to something without words. Is that all right with you?"

"Of course. Jazz or Classical?"

"How about something with a good beat?"

"I have just the thing," I said, as I went over to the stereo and located my David Sanborn "Change of Heart" album. I figured that would be wild enough for Melissa and Terri.

"By the way, how did you get into my apartment this afternoon? You really scared me when you did that."

"Sorry about that. I knocked, but you didn't answer. I thought you might be asleep or working in your room with the radio playing. I still had your spare set of keys from when I drove you to the hospital to see Dad, so I let myself in just as the phone rang. I laid your keys on the table by the phone, so I wouldn't walk off with them again."

"Terri should be here any minute," I said, peeking out between the curtains. I saw the old Catalina pull into a nearby parking space. As I watched Terri get out of the car, I noticed that a man in faded and tattered blue jeans and a dark gray T-shirt was watching her too. He was leaning against the phone booth next to the apartment complex office.

As soon as she got to my front door, I watched the man turn around, and pick up the telephone receiver. I hollered to Melissa to let Terri in and kept watching. At that moment the phone rang. As soon as Terri and Melissa were in the house, I said, "Lock the door behind you quickly." The phone rang a second time. Then I said, "If I'm not mistaken, that's our local mugger. Terri, answer the phone and pretend you're me. I think the guy is in the phone booth out there next to the office."

The phone rang again.

"Hello," Terri said in her normal voice.

"I see you have lots of company tonight," said the male voice at the other end of the telephone line.

Terri nodded to me, so I told her to hang up the phone. As soon as she did, I saw the guy in the phone booth hang up the phone. "Okay, that's got to be him. Call the police and tell them to come fast."

I described the man and his attire to Terri so she could tell the police. Meanwhile I kept watching the guy at the phone booth.

"If he calls again, try to keep him on the line until the police get here."

I stood there watching the guy smoke a cigarette, mentally willing him to call back. As soon as he crushed his cigarette butt into the ground, he turned around and picked up the phone.

"I think we've got him now. Get ready to answer it."

Sure enough, the phone rang again. Terri picked it up on the second ring, "Hello?"

"I'm surprised you answered again. I guess you're getting curious about me."

"Look, why are you bothering me? Don't you have anything better to do with your time?"

"I can't think of anything more fun than screwing a lesbian. Your kind really turns me on. I love to read about your wild sexual encounters in *Penthouse* when I'm at work."

"Oh please! You're talking about pornography, not real people. What makes you think I'm lesbian anyway?" Terri asked.

"I know you're a lesbian. I saw some of your drawings at an art show last summer. I really like your work. I even thought about buying a picture, but I didn't have any money at the time."

"Is that what you want? Money? Well, you're barking up the wrong tree, mister, because I don't have any money."

"I don't believe that. You're a famous artist, aren't you?"

Ignoring his question, Terri continued, "I don't know what you want, mister, but whatever it is, I'm not interested in helping you get it. So why don't you go fly a kite or something?"

"You know what I want, Elizabeth Higgins. I want your body. I want to make a woman out of you."

"What makes you think I would have anything to do with you?"

"You're talking to me, aren't you? You must be a little bit interested. Why don't you tell your friends to go home so we can be alone?"

"How do you know I have friends with me?

"Because I can see your apartment from where I am. I've been watching you all day. I see who goes in; I see who goes out. I saw you drive off with another queer today in an old car. I wouldn't mind making a woman out of her too. In fact, you can bring all your queer friends over, and I'll make women of all of them."

"Even my gay male friends?" Terri retorted sarcastically.

"Sure, why not? I'm not prejudiced."

"I can see that," Terri said, looking at me in desperation.

I whispered, "The police just pulled into the parking lot. Keep him talking, so he won't turn around and see them."

As soon as I said this, the guy in the phone booth looked over his shoulder, hung up the phone, and started walking away quickly. The patrol car stopped and a big, burly African-American policeman jumped out and started walking after the man. The man started to run, but the cop was too fast for him. Within seconds, he had the guy handcuffed and pinned to the patrol car.

While the burly policeman frisked the culprit, the other police officer, a stocky Caucasian woman with short brown hair, walked over to my apartment. She asked me if that was the man I had seen talking on the phone. I replied in the affirmative, and told her how he had called back after we had called them. She thought we were pretty smart to keep him distracted on the phone until they could get there. She asked us a bunch of questions, then wrote down all our names and telephone numbers, and went back to the patrol car. A few minutes later, the police car pulled away with the guy in the gray T-shirt in the back seat.

"I need a drink," Terri said after the police left. "I brought some champagne. Anybody here care to get smashed with me?"

"Sure. I've had enough drama for one day," I said, looking first at Terri then at Melissa.

Melissa said, "Wow! I've never had champagne before, but I'm willing to try something new."

"I'll go get some glasses," I said, wanting to do something that required physical energy. I had stood still at the front window for so long, I had begun to feel like a mannequin. Terri handed me the bottle of champagne on my way into the kitchen. As I came back out with three full glasses, I asked Terri to push the play button on the CD player. I had put the David Sanborn album in, but had not started it before all the excitement began. To Terri I said, "It's got a beat you can dance to."

"Good. Maybe we can all get drunk and dance ourselves silly. I almost feel as though I need to take a shower. I feel gross just having talked with that guy. He has some serious problems."

"I'm sorry. I guess I should have talked to him myself and let you keep watch. I didn't think of that before. When I spotted him watching you get out of your car, I knew right away that he was the guy. The only thing I could think to do was to keep an eye on him and wait for him to call.

Terri nodded once. "Well, it worked. I just hope they keep him in jail for a long time."

Melissa interjected, "Yeah, I hope they lock him up forever."

I laughed. "That's highly unlikely, but at least he should get the message that we don't want to have anything to do with him. I hope he can get some help. He must be really messed up psychologically." Then I held up my champagne glass and said, "To women. May we always be able to outsmart the oppressors."

"Here, here," Melissa responded then giggled her teenage giggle.

"For heaven's sake, Melissa," I laughed. "You haven't even drunk your first glass, and you've already started giggling. Just wait until you've had a few."

After we had all finished our first glass, I said, "I'd better go work on supper before I forget where the kitchen is."

"Oh, yeah. I forgot all about the vegetables that need to be chopped," Melissa added sheepishly.

"Don't worry about it. It shouldn't me take long to do it."

Terri followed me into the kitchen. "What are we having?"

"Nachos. I hope you like Mexican food."

"I like nearly everything. Is there anything for me to do?"

"Sure. You can sit here and talk to me while I chop up the vegetables."

"That sounds simple enough. I guess I should've brought tequila or margarita fixings."

"No, I think the champagne was a great idea,

especially since we have something to celebrate."

As I prepared the food, I asked Terri if she knew any lesbians who were Melissa's age. She couldn't think of anyone, but offered to call an acquaintance of hers who might know some younger, available women.

After I had put the pan of nachos under the broiler, Terri came up behind me, put her hands on my hips, and said, "So, are we going to dance our way to oblivion tonight, or shall I make another suggestion?"

"Suggest away."

The oven timer sounded, so I opened the door and pulled out the plate of steaming nachos. As soon as I had set the hot pan on the counter, Terri turned me around to face her.

"It's time, Liz."

"It is?"

Chapter Ten

As if on cue, Melissa walked into the kitchen before we got any closer. "Oh god, Liz, I'm so sorry," she said as we separated. "I'm going back into the living room. Call me when the coast is clear."

After she left, we tried to resume our former stance, but it was no use. The moment had been stolen once more. Terri and I looked at each other and laughed. Terri said, "What is this? Are you paying your little sister to drive me crazy? Are you two playing the team version of hard to get?"

I laughed at her jest. "Yes, Terri. The mugging and crank calls are part of it too. As well as the phone call to James. As a matter of fact, I designed the whole thing while I was checking out your body, right before you joined me on the elevator."

"You are creative. I stand in awe." She put her hands on her hips and shook her head at me.

"The food is getting cold."

Terri grinned. "That's okay. We can just put it next to my body, and it will warm up again."

"How about if I put myself next to your body so you can warm me up?"

"Is that a proposition?"

"It sounded distinctly like a proposition to me. Do you accept?"

"Definitely. How do we ditch your sister?"

"We don't. She's staying here tonight, but she won't mind. She can read a book. It isn't as though she doesn't know what we're up to."

Terri scowled. "That may be the worst part. I would feel as though there were a voyeur in the house."

"I'm sorry. Does that mean that you want to wait?"

"No, I have to go back to the hospital tomorrow night. I want to stay with you tonight, Elizabeth Higgins."

"I'm all yours."

She smiled. "I doubt that seriously, but I'll settle for a piece of you."

"Terri!" I said, shocked at her bluntness.

She laughed. "Well I didn't mean it that way. I just meant that we are just beginning to get to know each other, so I don't feel that I could possibly have all of you yet. I don't know who all of you is."

"Let's try to remedy some of that tonight. Are you ready to eat?"

"I suppose so. First things first."

I hollered towards the living room, "Melissa, it's safe to join us in the kitchen now."

As the three of us devoured the food, the conversation flowed smoothly. Throughout the entire meal I managed not to say anything stupid or eccentric. Maybe it was the effect of the champagne, or maybe it was the intensity of the last couple of days, but I began to feel as though I had known Terri for a long time. She told us about her upbringing in Maryland. I learned that her mother still lives in Baltimore and still works at the same restaurant where she started to waitress after Terri's father was killed.

I also discovered that, unlike Terri, my little sister cannot handle alcohol. As the evening wore on, Melissa got more and more giggly. Two glasses of champagne had given her a pretty good high. It was only about nine-thirty when she fell fast asleep on the couch. When I was convinced that she was out for the night, I retrieved the blanket and pillow she had used the night before. I covered her up and tucked her in. Then I motioned for Terri to follow me back to my bedroom.

I shut the door behind her then walked over to my radio and turned it on. It was tuned to the light jazz station. They were playing a song with a lot of mellow saxophone notes.

Terri looked around the room at the pictures on my wall, most of which was my work. "God, Liz, you're really good. How long have you been doing this kind of thing?"

"If you're referring to my artwork, I've been drawing seriously ever since junior high school. If you're referring to luring beautiful women into my bedroom, I've been at that less than ten years."

Terri laughed. "You're so witty, Liz. The way your mind works surprises me. I'm not used to being around people who joke about non-medical things. Medical humor is so predictable. You hear the same old lines all the time. I guess it's because doctors never get to go anywhere to learn new material. We just keep recycling the same old stupid jokes."

Terri walked over to my drawing table and looked down at the drawing pad that was lying open on my desk. "When did you draw this?" She asked, holding up my sketch of her sleeping figure.

"Last night when you fell asleep on my couch."

"No wonder you were sitting there staring at me."

"I had already finished drawing by the time you noticed anything. I had just settled down into a serious bout of aesthetic appreciation when you woke up."

She smiled guilelessly. "You say nice things."

"I mean them. I love to look at women, and I don't

mean in a lustful way. I just love the way women look." I like to drink in their beauty with my eyes.

"Are all of your exhibits of women?"

"No, I do other things too, though I have done exhibits that were entirely pictures of women or only nude women. I have a whole series of lesbian couples interacting with each other in different settings. One is of a couple of friends of mine. I was over at their house one night, and I drew them washing the dishes together. They thought it was funny, but touching too. I'll have to take you to see them some time. They live in Orlando. They've been together for over thirty years."

"Wow! That's a long time. I would like to meet them. I don't know many lesbian couples. Especially not ones that have been together that long."

"Would you like to see that picture?"

"Sure."

I pulled that particular drawing from my portfolio and handed it to Terri.

"I really like your work, Liz. You have a good eye for details."

"Thanks. I am very analytical, both visually and philosophically. I pick things apart in order to understand each tiny piece as well as they can be understood. Then I put it all back together again and try to see how the whole picture is made up of not just the individual pieces, but of the interplay of each piece with every other piece. You know how they tell you in mathematics that the whole is greater than the sum of the parts? Well, that's how I look at my subject when I draw it. That's also how I look at the world around me."

"I don't think I've ever thought that much about the world around me. Honestly, Liz, I feel as though I were born studying medicine. I have invested so much time into medicine that I sometimes forget that anything else exists."

"That's one reason I'm glad I didn't go into the field of medicine."

"Doesn't the business of being an artist ever get in the way of living your life?"

"Oh, sure. Especially when I'm handling the business end of an exhibition. That can turn into quite an all-consuming thing. I guess that's just how the worlds runs. Distort the beauty of art by turning it into the business of art."

Terri laughed suddenly. "Here I thought you were bringing me back here so we could make love. All we've done so far is analyze our lives."

"Perhaps that's not a bad thing."

"But you have to admit that it's a little different. So much for romance and mood setting."

Silence crept into the bedroom as we both sat on the edge of my bed lost in our thoughts. After a minute or two, I roused myself from my mental musings and decided it was time to shift the mood of the evening. I opened the drawer of my nightstand, pulled out a box of matches, and lit a candle.

Then I turned out the overhead light and said, "Shall we try once more for that kiss?" I put one hand on either side of Terri's soft face. I looked into her troubled eyes. "I'm sorry if I made you uncomfortable again. I get carried away sometimes."

Terri's troubled looked dissolved into one of tenderness and desire. "We may be very different, but I'm willing to try to bridge the gaps between us. You're an interesting person, Elizabeth Higgins, and I like what I see, even if I do get a little uncomfortable during our serious talks."

I pulled her body towards me, and she yielded to my embrace. I felt some of my fears melt away under the cover of the night. I was glad for the darkness and the lateness of the hour. My creative energy was peaking, and I knew that it would blend well with the sexual energy I felt surging within my breast.

"Terri?"

"Yes, Liz?"

"It's time."

"I know."

That was all we said for the span of an hour. At least, that was all we said with words. Our hands and bodies never ceased communicating curiosity, respect, timidity, and many other things, until at last, breathless and satisfied, we fell asleep in each other's arms.

Chapter Eleven

When I awoke the next morning, I found myself alone. A feeling of disappointment began to creep in, and I started trying to figure out what I had done wrong. I was just about to chide myself for getting my hopes up, when Terri walked back into the room and leaned against the doorway, smiling at me.

"Hi, Sleeping Beauty," she said with a tender smile.

"Please don't start that Sleeping Beauty stuff again. I'm quite aware that I look like a disaster in three dimensions when I first wake up."

"Liz, you do not. You're really quite beautiful, if you'd like to know what I think. Of course, if you're going to insist on playing the role of Cinderella's ugly stepsister, then I'll try not to interfere." She crossed her arms over her chest.

"I'm sorry. I guess I'm just a little insecure when I first wake up. I get this way whenever I'm not quite ready to face the world."

Terri shook her head a couple times slowly, smiling all the while. "You're such a bundle of contradictions, Liz. Sometimes you are so self-assured. Other times you're like a child who never gets enough attention. You start doing things that will evoke a response, positive or negative, out of any unsuspecting party who happens to be with you."

"Am I that bad?"

"Sometimes. But I don't mean it as a value judgment. I am just trying to make an observation. Will you do me a favor though?"

"What's that?"

"Will you please try not to deflect my compliments?"

"I'm sorry, Terri. You're right. I will try, but I may need some help remembering."

"Fair enough." Terri uncrossed her arms and walked across the room to where my easel stood.

I got out of bed, pulled on a T-shirt, and then shuffled off to the bathroom. When I returned, Terri was looking through my portfolio. She turned towards me as I walked into the room. "Are all these women former lovers?"

"Which ones?"

"The nudes."

I gave a little laugh. "No, some of them are people I don't even know. I'm pretty good at mentally undressing women."

"Oh? Do I look the way you pictured me?"

"Pretty much, though I wasn't expecting the cute little mole just above your pubic hairline."

"Oh please, don't remind me."

"I think it's very sexy."

"I'm glad someone does. I've always thought it was hideous."

"As for the women who are former lovers, there are three."

She glanced at me. "Let me see if I can pick them out."

"Okay, go ahead." I stood next to her and looked over her shoulder as she turned the pages of my portfolio.

Terri started back at the beginning of the nude series, looking very closely at each drawing. "Let me see. How about this one?"

"Yes, that's Marie."

"This one?"

"Nope, that one is from the cover of *Cosmopolitan.*"

"You read *Cosmopolitan*?

"No, but someone at my dentist's office does. That picture just caught my eye one day, so I borrowed their magazine for a few days."

"Okay, how about these two?"

"The first one is a no, but you guessed accurately with Kelly. She was my first lover."

"Kelly, huh? What about this one?"

"Yes."

"Does she have a name?" She lifted one eyebrow at me.

I nodded and said softly, "That's Aris."

"That's an interesting name. Is she really as beautiful as you portrayed her?

"She is."

"What happened to her?"

"She's still around."

"Oh yeah? Why did you break up?"

"I don't know exactly. I think we were both too perfectionist or something. She is the only one of the three who actually posed for their picture. The other two were drawn from memory."

"Could you draw me from memory?"

"Mostly, though I couldn't see you very well last night. Candlelight is not very illuminating, but I like the soft impressions it creates."

"Would you draw me if I offered to model?"

"Certainly. However, I must confess that I would probably draw you eventually, even if you didn't model."

She smirked. "I guess it can be dangerous to sleep with an artist."

"Definitely. However, I wouldn't exhibit it without

your approval."

"How decent of you. So how long would it take?"

"I could do a pretty good sketch within an hour. Then I could work on any remaining details from memory."

"Want to start today?"

"Sure. Shall I fix you some breakfast first?

"Sounds good to me. How about some coffee too?"

"Of course."

"Mind if I take a shower while it's cooking, or should I attempt to be inadequately helpful?"

I laughed. "No, go right ahead. I wasn't planning to do anything elaborate. There are towels in the linen closet in the hallway. Make yourself at home."

As I walked through the living room, I noticed that Melissa had gotten up, folded her blanket, and stacked pillow and blanket next to the couch. There was a note on the coffee table that read, "Liz, I got Robert to give me a ride to work. I'll see you later. Dad is coming home today, so I won't be staying here any more. Thanks a lot for letting me use your couch. I'm sorry if I made a nuisance of myself. I wasn't trying to. Lots of Love, Melissa."

I went into the kitchen and started the coffee. Then I began to prepare fried eggs and toast for my newly acquired lover and myself. As the aroma of brewing coffee permeated the apartment, a feeling of excitement came over me. I have always loved the smell of coffee brewing, even though I don't care much for drinking it. I associate that smell with my childhood. My mother always drank a couple cups of coffee in the morning. Dad never cared for it, so he stopped buying it after Mother disappeared.

The excitement of this childhood memory, coupled with the lovemaking of the night before, made me feel very good inside. I stood in the kitchen for a moment relishing the feeling, hoping it wouldn't fade too soon. Before I could totally lose myself in private reverie, the telephone rang. Startled by its sudden loudness, I snatched it up quickly. "Hello?"

"Is this Elizabeth Higgins?" A deep-toned, female voice asked.

"Yes, who's calling please?"

"This is Officer Pearcy of the Lakeland Police Department. I spoke with you last night."

"Yes, Officer. How may I help you?"

"We just wanted to let you know that the man we arrested yesterday is being held in our facility for the time being. I did want to warn you, however, that his lawyer is encouraging him to plea bargain, since he has no record of prior arrests. Should the judge accept the plea, our mugger will be free in a matter of months, possibly even weeks."

"How can that be? First he mugged me, and then he started stalking me. How can he be allowed to get away with that?"

"Easy, Ms Higgins. He didn't use a gun, and he's never done anything like this before, that we know of, at any rate. Believe me, this looks more like child's play to a judge who has sentenced murderers, armed robbers, and rapists."

"It certainly didn't seem like child's play to me!"

"No, I'm sure it didn't, which is why I'm calling to tell you this. I strongly advise you to invest in an answering machine and begin screening your calls. The judge is going to place a restraining order on Mr. Hardwick. That way, when he is released, he will be arrested immediately if he tries to contact you again. His voice on your answering machine is all we would need to pick him up again. He won't even be allowed to set foot on the property of your apartment complex."

"Well, that's something at least. I appreciate your calling me, Officer . . ."

"Pearcy. And you're welcome, Ms. Higgins."

"So will I need to testify against him in court?"

"I don't think so, but we'll let you know. We have your written statement and the statement of your doctor friend. Plus we were able to trace some of the calls he made from the telephone booth outside your apartment complex, including the one he made as we were on our way there. The guy's an idiot for staying on the phone so long. It's as though he wanted us to catch him. Either that, or he has no clue as to how long it takes to trace a telephone call these days."

"To be frank with you, Officer, he didn't seem to be a very intelligent person. His conversational skills were about junior high level, so it doesn't surprise me that he's a stupid criminal."

"You'd be surprised at just how stupid some criminals are. At least the ones that get caught."

"So this guy has never assaulted anyone before?"

"I didn't say that. I only said that he's never before been caught at it. He, of course, claims that he has never done it before."

"Why did he do it this time then? Why did he choose me to be his first victim?"

"According to him, it was just a spur of the moment thing. He was walking home from his job at a nearby convenience store, when he saw you in the parking lot by yourself. He said that at first he was just going to try to talk with you because you were 'such a babe'—pardon me, those were his words—but you were totally oblivious to his presence when he walked up. So he decided to whack you on the head with the Coke bottle he had in his hand and steal your money."

"Oh great. So I was victim of a bored convenience store worker, who thought he would try to pick me up?"

"Looks like it, though the way he talked about you, and the way he spoke to you on the phone, says to me that what he thought about doing originally was more like sexual assault. Of course we can't prove that, since he didn't follow through with it."

"Thank goodness for that!"

"Definitely. Well, I won't take up any more of your time, Ms. Higgins. I just wanted to let you know how things were progressing in your case. Feel free to give me a call if you have a question about it. I have your case number, if you'd like to make a note of it. It's L-77523."

"Wait! Let me grab a pen." I read the number back to her to make sure I'd written it down correctly. She also gave me the number for the dispatcher in case I needed to reach her.

After she had verified the information, Officer Pearcy said, "Just leave a message if I'm not in. I'll give you a call back as soon as I can."

"I really appreciate your help, Officer. Did you say that were you one of the officers who arrested the mugger?"

"Yes, but it was my partner, Ned Simmons, who physically apprehended the guy. Hardwick didn't stand a chance with Ned."

"I know. I watched the whole scene from my apartment window. Your partner was quite impressive. Made me glad I wasn't a criminal."

"Yeah, he used to be a world class body builder. He's definitely not someone to mess with. I'm grateful to have him for a partner. I think that his physical presence scares the crap out of most people. It certainly keeps punks from harassing me."

"Is that something that happens a lot to other women on the police force?"

"Oh, sure. I used to have problems with that occasionally before they teamed me up with Ned. But I won't bore you with all the details. Take care of yourself, Ms. Higgins. And buy yourself that answering machine before that creep gets out."

"I will. Thanks. Say, I know you're busy with other cases, but could you give me a call if he does get released?"

"Sure, if I hear about it. I may not know about it right away though. You might just want to call me in about a month. That will remind me to check up on it."

"Okay. I'll do that. Thanks again for the warning. I really appreciate your taking time to call me."

"No problem. We try to get back to people when we can. Anyway, take good care of yourself, Ms. Higgins, and give me a call soon."

"Thanks, I will. Goodbye."

As I hung up the phone, Terri came out of the bathroom, still toweling her wet hair. "Who was that on the phone?"

"That was Officer Pearcy, one of the cops who arrested the mugger yesterday. His name, by the way, is Hardwick, though she didn't tell me his first name."

"She?"

"Officer Pearcy."

"Oh, so it wasn't the linebacker who tackled the obscene phone caller? That guy was amazing!"

"No, it was the other one. The woman who came

into the apartment and filled out the report."

"Ah yes, she's the same one I talked to at the hospital. I had a hard time keeping her out of the emergency room when you were unconscious. So what did she have to say?"

"She wanted me to know that Hardwick might not stay in jail long, so I should get an answering machine."

She stopped toweling her hair and looked at me with a puzzled expression. "Why? That doesn't quite make sense."

"Apparently he doesn't have a police record, so his lawyer is going to cop a plea. If the judge goes for it, Hardwick will walk in a few months or weeks even."

"God, Liz, you sound like a lawyer. I didn't know you could talk like that."

"You forget that my big brother is a lawyer. I can talk legalese with the best of them, if I want to. Just don't ask me how to talk like a CPA. Stanley always puts me to sleep when he talks about his job. At least James' career choice is interesting sometimes."

"Is he a criminal lawyer?"

"No, actually he's a corporate lawyer, but he can make even a corporate case sound interesting."

"A regular John Grisham, huh?"

"Okay, so he's not that interesting, though he did have a case that involved the Mafia once."

"Really?"

"Yeah, it got kind of hairy for awhile. He received a couple death threats while it was going on."

"So what happened?"

"He lost. The Mafia's lawyer was just too slick for him. Or for his senior partner. He was really only assisting on that case."

Terri twirled her towel into a rope and flicked it

my way without making contact. "Or they got to him."

"What?"

"The Mafia. Maybe they got to your brother and his partner, so they didn't offer a stronger case."

"Will you stop that? First you get me all worked up about my mother then we have this mugger guy, and now you're trying to tell me that my brother buckled under the pressure of thugs. What next, Terri?"

She held up her free hand as if to ward off a physical blow. "I was just kidding, Liz. Besides I didn't have anything to do with the mugging. It just happened to occur in the parking lot of my hospital."

"True. But it seems as though I had a quiet life up until I met you in the hospital. Now suddenly my life and my family's lives are shrouded in intrigue."

"Hey, that's hardly fair! My life has been pretty calm up until I met you too. Now it seems as though all hell has broken loose. It was your mother who vanished years ago without a trace. It was you who got mugged. It was your brother who was involved with the Mafia."

"He wasn't involved with the Mafia! He was involved in a legal battle that included some members of the Mafia. There's a difference."

"Objection sustained, counselor. Anyway I was just making the point that this sudden twist of events in your life doesn't really have anything to do with me. Most of this stuff happened long before I arrived on the scene. Years before."

"Terri?"

"Yes, Liz?"

"Are we fighting?"

"No. We aren't fighting. We're just having a

difference of perspective."

"That seems to be a recurring theme in our relationship up to this point."

"It does, doesn't it? I guess maybe it's because we're just getting to know one another."

"Yeah. That must be what it is."

Crushed by the weight of our introspection, the conversation ground to a painful halt. To avoid the emotional panic that was about to seize me, I changed the subject. "So what do you say about a little coffee? Surely that machine has stopped dripping by now."

"Good idea!" Terri responded a little too enthusiastically. "Let me go hang up this towel, run a comb through my hair, and I'll be right back."

I went into the kitchen, poured two cups of coffee, and then set myself to the task of finishing the breakfast preparations that had been interrupted by Officer Pearcy's call. As I worked, I thought about all the different choices women have now in regards to employment. I had just spoken with a female police officer. I am dating a female physician, and I myself am an artist.

I mourned the fact that my mother had been excluded from such opportunities in her youthful days. Her limitations in life were the unfortunate by-products of the post-war era. When she was young, women were greatly discouraged from seeking a career outside the home. She was born too late to have experienced the freedom women had during World War II, when they were forced to go to work to keep the country going. Yet she was born too soon to have benefited greatly from the Women's Liberation Movement of the 1970's. By the time women starting burning their bras, my mother was already imprisoned by her lack of education and opportunity. Not to mention several children and a controlling, yet seemingly helpless, husband. What a different woman she might have been had she been born in a later decade.

I pondered what type of career she might have had if she had been born later. I had to admit that it was hard to picture her in any role other than that of a mother and wife. My clearest memories of her revolve around my coming home from school to the aroma of fresh baked cookies, cakes, and pies. My mother had truly been a Betty Crocker kind of woman. Forever swaddled in an apron. Forever chained to the kitchen.

I still loved my mother, but I also realized that my love was directed only towards some faded old photographs and an equally faded memory of her warm embrace. I could not honestly say that I knew Constance Higgins, so how could I truly love her for herself? I didn't even know if she were still alive. If James hadn't heard from her in years, then there was no telling where she might be now.

As the tears began to well up in my eyes, I realized that it was futile to try to regain the person who had been my mother. She was gone from my life, probably forever. There was no sense in trying to bring her back. If she had wanted to be part of my life now, then she would be here. So, either she didn't wish to share the lives of her children, or she was dead. Neither of which was a very cheerful thought. As a large tear, filled with self-pity, began rolling down my cheek, I felt Terri's arms encircle me.

"Hey, I didn't know making breakfast was such a depressing task. Had I known, I wouldn't have left you to do it all by yourself. Are you all right?"

I turned around to face Terri then buried my head in her shirt. "I'm sorry, I've just been thinking about my mother. Wondering where she is and if I'll ever see her again."

"Oh, Liz. I'm so sorry I opened up this wound. I never would've said anything about it, if I had known it was going to cause you such pain. Sometimes I just get all involved in the moment and don't realize the consequences of my actions. I've always been like that. It has gotten me into loads of trouble. On the other hand, it's probably the reason why I had the guts to kiss my first girlfriend, so I suppose it's not all bad. Will you forgive me for sticking my nose into your family business?"

"There's nothing to forgive, Terri. You didn't do anything wrong. I'm an emotional wreck right now, I guess. With everything that has happened lately, I feel so exposed, so vulnerable. At a time in my life when I could really use a mother or father to turn to, I find that I have only a ghost of a mother and a beast for a father. My perspective of my whole family has been radically changed in the past few days. Not only is my father sick and weak right now, but I've learned that he was unfaithful and unkind to my mother. I'm finding it difficult not to hate him right now."

"I can understand that. I think I'd feel the same way in your circumstances. I'm really sorry that your mother didn't at least stay in contact with you kids, but I suppose she couldn't, if she needed to avoid your father. I feel really bad for the woman. It's too bad we can't track her down somehow. I don't suppose the Lakeland Police could be of any help. God, listen to me running off at the mouth again. Just forget I said anything. I will try my best to think before I speak, especially when it comes to your family situation. I'm sorry, Liz. I can be such an idiot sometimes."

"Now who's being overly critical of herself? You're not saying anything I haven't already thought about. I'm just not sure I want to know what happened to her right now. I may even be angry with her. I can understand her leaving my father, but I can't understand her leaving her children without a word of communication all these years. Surely she could have figured out some way to communicate with us. To let us know she was alive."

"I suppose so. Still, it's hard to know her perspective."

"Well, let's eat before everything gets cold. We may need to reheat our breakfast in the microwave. See if it's hot enough for you."

"It's fine, as far as I'm concerned. I seldom get to eat a hot breakfast anyway." She took a bite of her fried eggs. "Yum, this is divine."

"Thanks, though I suppose it's not hard to compete with hospital food."

We munched our toast and eggs in relative silence, each of us caught up in our private thoughts. When we were finished with our breakfast, I rinsed off the dishes and stuck them in the dishwasher.

"So what time do you have to go to work tonight?"

"Not until ten."

"Did you have any plans for today?"

"Not anything in particular. What about you? Do you ever work in the daytime?"

"Sometimes I do, if it strikes my fancy, or if I have an impending deadline I need to meet for an exhibition. But I'm not planning to do anything today. I think I need some rest and time off. I'm really feeling very raw emotionally."

"Do you still want to draw me, or is that too much like work?"

"Oh no, that would be pure pleasure, rest assured. Disrobe at will, unless you would like me to draw you clothed."

"I don't mind posing in the nude as long as you're the artist, and the blinds are closed."

"Then I'll be back shortly with my tools. I'll expect to see some soft womanly flesh when I return."

"How you do talk, you lecherous artist-type!"

I exited the living room with a fiendish flourish of my arms.

Chapter Twelve

When I returned with my drawing tools, I found Terri lying on the floor in a seductive pose, partly on her side and partly on her stomach. It was a perfect pose. Exposing nothing that could be viewed as X-rated, yet tantalizing to the senses. Every womanly curve was on display, carefully positioned to reveal maximum beauty. In that pose, she definitely didn't strike me as looking much like a doctor. She looked much more like a classical sculpture of a Greek Goddess. I made myself comfortable on the couch. "My, but don't you look like the Goddess of Love."

She smiled sweetly. "Thanks. Flattery will get you everywhere. Not that there are many places on my body that you haven't been."

"Perhaps, but I'm quite willing to go on another exploratory adventure, if you'll let me. I'm sure there must be some territory I've left uncharted. Opportunity awaits the willing adventurer."

"My, but don't you sound like an opportunist."

"I am an opportunist. And come to think of it, you have the most delicious opportunity knockers."

Terri laughed. "I cannot believe Elizabeth Higgins just said that! You truly are a lewd and lecherous artist-type. I was just kidding before, but now I know it's true."

"Have I shocked you? You don't seem like a woman who would be easily shocked."

"I'll admit that you surprised me there. But then, I've been startled by your wit since the very beginning. Sometimes you're so serious. Then you come up with these unexpected quips. Those two aspects of your personality seem a little incongruent to me."

"Yes, I suppose they do seem a little odd. What can I say? I've always been the queer one in the family."

Terri groaned at my pun. "I surrender! No more puns. I can't take any more." She rolled over onto her back in mock agony. The sudden revelation of a full frontal view made me catch my breath.

"Mm. Suppose we do a little research before I get to work? Call it an anatomical study, if you will. You are absolutely stunning, Terri."

I slid off the couch onto the floor beside my naked model. I began nibbling on her adorable little ears.

Terri lifted her head and looked at me very seriously. "Your little sister isn't going to appear suddenly out of nowhere, is she?"

"God, I hope not. No, come to think of it, she's out with Robert and isn't supposed to be coming back here tonight. Dad's going home tonight, so she'll be with him. I think we're safe."

"Good! I'm not in the mood to be interrupted again. Playing hard to get is one thing, but this lustus interruptus is quite another."

"Lustus interruptus? Are you serious? That's not really a term, is it?"

Terri smiled impishly. "It is now. It's amazing what a little Latinizing can do for a conversation. Paints a vivid picture, huh? But I'm serious. Just when I'm ready to turn on the passion full throttle, your little sister pops up. Except in your bedroom last night, of course. And look how rewarding those moments of privacy were."

"I remember. But don't worry. Even if she does show up, she doesn't have a key, so she can't get in if we don't let her in. She'll get the hint, if I don't answer the door."

"Great! Now what was it you were doing to my ear?" She turned her head to allow me better access to her ears.

Just as I began nibbling on Terri's adorable ear, the phone rang. "I'm not going to answer it. I really need to get an answering machine."

"Are you sure you don't want to answer that?"

"Quite sure. Now let me see. Where was I? Oh yes, I remember, those cute little ears of yours."

As I began to nibble on her neck and ears, Terri relaxed in my arms and fell into some serious moaning. The sound of the ringing telephone quickly faded from our awareness as our bodies gradually grew more and more intertwined. I paused in my exploration of Terri's body just long enough to disengage myself from my clothes. Terri had been busy unbuttoning and unzipping me, while I had been sampling her neck and breasts.

"You feel so good next to me, Liz. You make me forget the clinical aspects of examining a body. When I'm with you, I'm completely absorbed in you. So... mm, oh, my. Oh, Liz."

As the conversation dwindled to moans and groans, pleasure expanded to fill the relative silence. After a couple hours of vigorous lovemaking, we both fell asleep on the floor. Smiles on our faces; satisfaction in our hearts. The next thing I'm aware of is the sound of Terri's voice talking to someone on the telephone.

"Hi. Yeah, this is Terri. I'm going to be a little late tonight. I was so wiped out from that last shift I totally crashed this afternoon. I'm going to get a quick shower, grab a bite to eat, and be right there.

Thanks. I really appreciate it. Sorry. See you later."

As she hung up the phone, I sat up and looked at her. "What time is it? Did we oversleep?"

"Yeah. It's a little after nine. I've got about thirty minutes to get cleaned up, eat, and drive over there. I won't be too late. God, I can't believe I slept that long. I seldom sleep for more than four hours at a stretch. I must've been exhausted."

"Or contented." I smiled.

"There is that. Oh well, they'll just have to survive without me for a few minutes. Can I borrow your shower?"

"Sure. Don't you need something to wear?"

"Not too worry. I have a clean pair of scrubs in the car. That's one of the advantages of working in a hospital. You don't have to have much of a wardrobe. Good thing too. I don't have many clothes. All my money has been going towards my education for more years than I can count."

"I'll go get your clothes while you shower. Where are your keys?"

"On the kitchen table, I think. Thanks."

"Sure. Want something to eat here?"

"No, I'll just stop somewhere on the way in. That way I can eat and drive at the same time. That'll save time."

"Okay."

As I stepped outside to get Terri's clothes out of her car, I had a moment of panic. I tried to reassure myself that there was no one out here waiting to pounce on me. Hardwick was in jail. Everything should be okay. Yet even with those mental reassurances, I felt uneasy. I couldn't shake the feeling that someone was watching me. I got the scrubs out of the car as quickly as possible, which wasn't very quick because I forgot about Terri's broken door. I had to shut it half a dozen times before I could get it to stay shut. Then I nearly ran back into the apartment.

Terri was just coming out of the bathroom. She was vigorously rubbing her head with a towel. "Are you all right, Liz? You look pale."

"Yes, I think so. It's stupid really. I just got scared being outside by myself in the dark. I've never been afraid of the dark before."

"Let me leave you my pager number. I wish I didn't have to leave you alone so soon after everything that's happened, but I have to go to work. Please call me though, if you need to talk. I may not be able to return your call immediately, but I will call back as soon as I can."

"Thanks. I'll be okay. I'm much better now that I'm back inside. I just felt extremely exposed all the sudden. I've never felt that way before about going outside at night."

"Maybe not, but it's perfectly understandable considering the circumstances. Have you ever thought about taking a self-defense class? That might help you feel better."

"No, I haven't, but that's not a bad idea."

"Well, I'd better go. You're sure you're going to be all right? Shall I try to track down Melissa and see if she can come over?"

"No, really, I'm fine. Once I get to work, I'll forget all about it."

"Saying that, I guess we're going to have to reschedule my modeling session for my next day off. Which is Wednesday, in case you're interested."

"God yes, I'm interested. We did get a little distracted, didn't we?"

"Yes, but what a lovely way to get distracted! You're a wonderful lover, Liz. I'll call you when I go on break. You'll be up, right?"

"Undoubtedly. Bye!"

Terri leaned over and kissed me sweetly on the lips. "Hmm. I've never wanted to play hooky from work so badly in all my life."

"I know the feeling. See you later, sexy doctor."

"See you later, lustful artist-type."

I closed the door behind Terri then watched through a gap in the curtains as she got in her clunker and drove away.

Suddenly alone again in my quiet apartment, I had a fleeting moment of panic. I walked over to the stereo and turned on the radio. I gathered up the scattered articles of clothing on the living room floor and threw them into the laundry basket in my bedroom. Then I collected my drawing supplies with the intention of drawing Terri from memory. Instead I started thinking about what she said about a self-defense class.

I pulled the phone book from its hiding place under the end table and perused the yellow pages for a place that offered classes for women. There were lots of martial arts classes available, but what I really wanted was simply self-defense. I had no desire to get a black belt in body bludgeoning. Then I wondered if I shouldn't just call the police to see if they knew about anything like that. Surely they would. Didn't they have to deal with victims of crime on a daily basis?

I found the phone number Officer Pearcy have given me and dialed it. When the dispatcher answered, I said, "Hello? I'm trying to reach Officer Pearcy."

The male voice on the other end of the line indicated that Officer Pearcy was on patrol, but that he would give her a message for me. I gave him my name and phone number then hung up the phone. I decided to try again to work on my sketch of Terri. This time I was able to concentrate a little better. I did a rough sketch in pencil then pondered where to go from there. I wondered if pastels would be a good medium for Terri. But then I thought of those dark eyes of hers and decided on charcoal instead.

The ringing of the phone at ten-thirty startled me. "Hello?"

"Is this Elizabeth Higgins?"

"May I ask who's calling?"

"This is Officer Pearcy with the Lakeland Police Department. I got a message that you called a little while ago. I wanted to return your call as quickly as possible. Am I calling too late?"

"Officer Pearcy! No, no. It's not too late for me. I'm always up late. I was just a little startled by the phone ringing. I was rather deep in concentration at the time."

"I hope I didn't take you away from something important."

"No, you're fine. I was just working on a sketch. I'm glad you called. I was wondering if you had any information about self-defense classes for women. I, um, I've been feeling rather ..."

"Vulnerable?"

"Well, actually, yes. That's exactly it."

"I'm not surprised. It's a normal response for attack victims. As a matter of fact, I do know about a self-defense class for women. I teach it myself. I started it about a year ago. I kept having women in similar situations calling the department with the same kinds of questions. Most of the time we just referred them to the martial arts businesses, but so many of those are male-oriented. I wanted to find a place where women could go and learn self-defense techniques in an all woman environment. I figured they would feel more comfortable in that setting, which would then help them to learn more from the whole experience."

"Let me guess. You didn't find anything like it, so you started your own?"

"Precisely. There's nothing wrong with what the martial arts businesses are teaching. They just have a different focus than what I thought would be good for female attack victims. I mean, some of these women have been brutalized by men. The last thing they need is to be involved in aggressive bodily contact with them."

"But if it's an all woman group, how do we learn to defend ourselves against male attackers?"

"The first several sessions deal with finding our personal power and about learning how not only to use it physically when necessary, but how to use it psychologically so it doesn't become necessary to use it physically. Towards the end of the sessions, Ned, my partner, comes in to lend a hand. In order to help the women feel less intimidated by his powerful appearance, I make him wear a pink tutu to class. You just wouldn't believe the difference it makes in these women. It's hard to be intimidated by a man in a pink tutu. I don't care how big and ferocious he may look otherwise. Then later he comes in street clothes, but the women have already seen him in his other attire, so they have an easier time viewing him as non-threatening."

"It's very empowering for women to learn how to

fend off someone as huge and powerful as Ned. Rarely will they be called upon to defend themselves against a bigger or stronger opponent. But in their minds, he's just a big guy in a pink tutu. This mental image helps them to disarm all men on the streets. I teach them to visualize all men in pink tutus. You'd be surprised how much that strips men of their psychological power over these women."

"My god, that's sounds wonderful! I can't believe that big hunk of police officer puts on a pink tutu for that class. How on earth did you convince him to do it?"

"Oddly enough, it was his idea first. Though when he realized he was talking about something he was going to have to do, he started back-pedaling in a big hurry. But I knew I had him then. The words came out of his mouth, and I wouldn't let him back out. It was rather comical at the time."

"I'll bet."

"What was really comical was trying to find a pink tutu big enough to fit Ned. In the end I had to call on his sister's sewing talents to make it for us. She had a blast fitting him for it."

"Ned must be one special man to have the nerve to do wear such an unmasculine outfit. I don't think I know any men who would dare to do such a thing."

"Yeah, Ned's a great guy. No better partner around, as far as I'm concerned."

"Is he married?"

"No. Why? Are you interested?"

I chuckled. "No, just curious."

"Oh come on. Why not? He's a great guy!"

"Obviously, but he's not my type.'

"Now how do you know that? You've never even talked to him, have you?"

"He's not my type because he's a man. I'm lesbian."

"Oh, well, I can certainly see how that might pose a problem."

"But you've convinced me to join your class. When and where do you hold them?"

"We hold them at the YWCA. Do you know where that is?"

"I think so. I haven't been by there in awhile, but I'm sure I can find it."

"I've got a class that is winding up this Tuesday night. Then I take a break from it for a couple weeks. So if you're interested, plan on it two weeks from now. But if you'd like to sit in on the final meeting of this last session, you can. That way you can check it out before you decide to register. It starts at seven."

"I should be able to make it. Thanks. You've been a tremendous help."

"That's what I'm here for. 'To serve and to protect.' Well, I hope to see you Tuesday night."

"Okay. Thanks again."

"Don't mention it, Ms Higgins. Take care and good-bye."

"Bye."

I placed the phone back on the receiver and made a mental note to attend that self-defense class.

I decided to call Terri to let her know about the class, but when I dialed her number, she was unavailable. I left a message with the person on the phone then went back to work on my sketch. I was deeply into my work again by the time the phone rang again. I was so startled by the loud ringing that I literally jumped up to answer it.

"Hello?"

"You rang for a doctor?"

"Terri! Good, it's you."

"Well now, who else were you expecting?"

"No one. I was lost in my drawing of you, and I was completely oblivious to anything else in the world. But drawing you was also making me miss you."

"Is this another drawing of me, or the one you did on the couch?"

"It's a new one. I'm trying to capture the pose you had this afternoon."

"Does that mean I won't get to pose for it?"

"Oh no, I will need you again, so I can work on the details."

"Ah, I think I get the picture, so to speak. You'll need a closer examination in order to finish the work."

"Do you object?"

"None whatsoever. In fact, I look forward to it. I just wish I didn't have to wait until Wednesday night."

"Tell me about it. But listen, I wanted to let you know that I took your advice about the self-defense idea. I called Officer Pearcy to see if she knew of any classes, and you'll never guess what she said."

"I'm clueless. What did she say?"

"She teaches a self-defense class for women on Tuesday evenings. She invited me to attend the last session of the series that ends this week."

"That's great, Liz! I'm really glad you called her. I'm sure it will make you feel better."

"Me too. The way she described the class, it sounded as though it would be fun, as well as helpful. I'm kind of excited about it."

"Well, good. Listen, I need to get back, but I'll call you on my break, if you think you'll be up around two."

"I should be. Obviously if I'm not, I won't answer the phone. But after that lengthy nap this afternoon, I should be awake until at least three. Besides I'm really into this drawing of you. It's almost as good as being with you."

"I don't think I like the sounds of that."

"Well, let's just say that's it the next best thing."

"That sounds a little better. Gotta go! I'll talk to you later."

"I'll be here, no doubt."

I hung up the phone then went into the kitchen to put on the tea kettle. I carried my sketchpad with me and sat down in the breakfast nook to wait for the kettle to whistle. I propped the sketch up on the counter to get a good look at it from afar. It was shaping up nicely.

After a cup of chamomile tea, and another round of sketching, I fell asleep on the couch. When the phone rang at two in the morning, I reached up and answered it in a groggy voice."

"Hello?"

"Liz? Are you awake? You don't sound very awake."

"Yeah, I think so. I wasn't though."

"I'm sorry. I didn't mean to wake you. I was hoping you'd be doing your night owl routine."

"I think it was the hot tea that did it. Or maybe it's just all the passionate lovemaking we've been doing lately. That always makes me sleep more."

"Isn't that strange? I get more energetic."

"Oh yeah? You weren't very energetic yesterday afternoon when we passed out on the floor."

"Perhaps not, but I am now. I've been flying around this hospital. One of my fellow doctors asked me if I'd just gotten laid. He's never seen me so happy."

"And what did you tell him?"

"Nothing, of course. I just smiled and flitted down the hallway, leaving him to wonder."

"Good tactic."

"Yes, I thought so. It's better to keep them guessing."

"Do your colleagues know you're lesbian?"

"I suppose some of them have guessed as much, though I haven't made a point of advertising it. I don't wish to be judged by my sex life. That's personal to me. My professional work is what needs to be evaluated."

"I take it the medical world isn't very tolerant of such deviance?"

"I think not, though I don't try to hide it either. If someone asked me, I would tell the truth. If they don't like it, then too bad. I would just hate for someone to evaluate my work based on my sexual orientation. If they don't know, it isn't a factor."

"Do you think it would hinder your career if it were known?"

"I don't know. I haven't given it much thought. It hasn't really been an issue for me up until now. When I was in medical school, I didn't have time for a love life. Now I barely do. If they find out, then I'll have to deal with the consequences, if there are any. In the meantime, when I'm at work, I'm at work. When I'm at home, I'm at home. I'd rather keep those two aspects of my life separate."

"I guess that's where my life is so different from yours. Who I am at home is who I am at work. There is no line of demarcation. I am what I do. I do what I am."

"Sounds like the lyrics to a new song."

I giggled. "Maybe a really bad one."

"Hmm, you're probably right about that. Well, I've got to get back to work. I hope you can go back to sleep."

"Yeah, or go back to work myself. It's a flip of the coin right now. I'm still kind of tired."

"Go to sleep, Liz. I'll talk to you tomorrow some time. I won't call early."

"Bye."

I hung up the phone and promptly fell back to sleep.

Chapter Thirteen

It was pouring down rain when I pulled into the driveway of the YWCA on Tuesday night. I found a parking space as close to the entrance as possible, shut the car off, and grabbed my umbrella. I jumped out of the car and locked it as quickly as I could then, with umbrella unfurled, ran to the front entrance. It was raining hard at a forty-five degree angle, so by the time I got there, I was completely drenched in spite of the umbrella. It was a typical Florida downpour at an untypical time of the year. The state was getting battered by a storm that had stalled just off the coast. It was the kind of storm that shouldn't form in December, but somehow had. The air felt balmy enough to be September. It was a fluke storm, the radio announcer had said. But fluke or not, it had gotten me just as wet.

I shook the bulk of the water off my umbrella and returned it to its little plastic sack. According to standard Sunshine State protocol, there were no umbrella stands at the front door. Most Floridians just wait until the downpour passes or they get wet. Umbrellas aren't really all that helpful anyway. I was a case in point.

If you're going to be out in a Florida downpour, then you'd better be covered from head to toe in vinyl. Though usually a Florida downpour includes lots of thunder and lightning. This storm was no exception. Generally in a thunderstorm, I try to stay indoors, since I have no desire to become a lightning strike victim. I have never figured out why some people stay outside, playing football, having a picnic, or whatever, while a storm like this one is around.

Even if it isn't raining much, the lightning is still there and still very dangerous. Yet people continue to hang around outside, while lightning is crackling nearby, even though Florida averages a hundred lightning fatalities a year, allowing it the dubious distinction of being number one in that category in the United States.

As I entered the building, I followed the maze-like hallway to the room where the self-defense class was being held. There were small handmade signs pointing the way, as though I might not be the only one who would be clueless as to its exact whereabouts. A glance at my watch revealed that I was five minutes late, though from the sounds in the hallway behind me, I wasn't the only one. As I reached for the doorknob, three women rounded the corner behind me and greeted me in low voices. A sense of shared guilt at being late drew us close together as we entered the room en masse.

Before we could locate a seat, Officer Pearcy boomed in her strong contralto voice, "Well, hello ladies! I was just about to begin our final session. I'm glad to see you all made it. Ms. Higgins, welcome! I'm glad you found the place." Her smile was so warm it nearly dried my soggy clothes.

I smiled back and mumbled my thanks as I plopped myself down on the edge of one of the many exercise mats that covered the floor of the classroom.

"As I started to say, tonight's the night we pull together everything we've learned over the past eight weeks. My partner Ned will be here shortly. Tonight we get to pummel him, with padding of course, in his street clothes. No more pink tutus, though I hope you will continue to keep that image firmly embedded in your mind. He may be playing the part of a thug, but he's a thug in a pink tutu. It is a mental game that can help you to disarm men psychologically. As long as we feel and act intimidated by men, they will continue to harass and victimize us. Change the mindset, and you will change the way you interact with them. That includes bosses, boyfriends, fathers, brothers, as well as the lowlife on the street who thinks you are flattered by his wolf whistles. How many of those guys do you think would mess with women who know, and act like they know, that they are powerful beings?

"I've said it before, and I'll say it again. Men are afraid of women who know how to use their personal power. Statistics have shown that women who dress a certain way, walk a certain way, act a certain way, are more likely to be targets of sexual or physical harassment. And I'm not necessarily talking about dressing like a quote, unquote floozy. I'm talking about the difference between power dressing, power walking, power acting, and the scared rabbit mentality. Yes, you need to use common sense. Men can act like animals if you dress seductively. But they're less likely to, if you act, walk, and look as though you know who you are, know where you're going, and know how to get there. It's an attitude, ladies, and you can wear that attitude in a bathing suit, if you have to. And in this state, you just may have to. Women are sometimes attacked on the beaches, though more frequently at night than in broad daylight. Some of the more secluded beaches, however, are prime places for attack even in daylight."

"I know of one particularly place on the east coast, just south of New Smyrna where two young college women were walking together along a mostly deserted beach. Suddenly a man who was wearing absolutely no clothes walked right up to them and started a conversation. Now one of these women had been in my class, and she put into practice some of the things she learned in this class."

"First of all, she put a pink tutu on him. In her mind, this big hairy guy with his dick hanging down, all big and swollen, was just another clown in a pink tutu. She mentally covered up his weapon, which in this case was his penis. Now ladies, here's a guy with a lot of balls, so to speak. He walks up to these women with his dick hanging out in full view. That's like someone walking up to you with a gun in his hand. That dick was meant to be a weapon. When these two young women used their personal power to disarm him, in this case, acting as though he wasn't standing there with his stuff hanging out, he was at a loss."

"They were perfectly calm and acted as though there was absolutely nothing unusual about the situation. What a psychological blow—excuse the pun. They spoke ever so curtly to his face then politely excused themselves and walked back to where their friends were waiting for them. Then, of course, they were smart enough to leave together in a group. They didn't wait around for anything else to happen."

One woman raised her hand.

Officer Pearcy nodded in her direction. "Yes, Marcie?"

"Did they call the police?"

"They did not. The man had not committed a crime. It's a private, isolated beach, which is I believe, clothing optional. So what that man did could be construed as perfectly harmless. Yet these two women were smart enough to assume that here was a potentially dangerous situation, and therefore, the best thing to do was to get out of there as quickly as they could. If you feel uncomfortable in a situation, there's usually a good reason for it, even if you don't find out what it is."

I tried to picture the scene in my head and couldn't help but giggle to myself. Apparently I wasn't the only one getting a kick out of the mental picture, as I heard several women snickering and talking quietly amongst themselves.

Officer Pearcy continued. "It is rather funny. Even the women involved thought so afterwards, though they were somewhat shaken up by the encounter. They realized how close they had come to being sexually victimized. In fact, they both felt somewhat victimized psychologically. On one hand they felt empowered by their success. Yet they also realized that the situation could have turned out differently."

Just then Ned entered the room. He was wearing baggy sweatpants and an oversized T-shirt. Underneath his clothes he had thick pads strapped to his body for protection. He smiled at the class and waved. Most of the women smiled back warmly. You could tell by the atmosphere in the room that he had managed to make himself accepted by these women. There was no sense of fear amongst the women of the group. There was more a sense of camaraderie. There was no powerful man in the room—just a big guy in an imaginary pink tutu. Even though Liz had never seen him in his ballerina garb, she had no trouble envisioning him in it. It made her smile.

"Greetings, fair ballerina!" Officer Pearcy bellowed.

Ned grinned at her then made a terrible attempt at a pirouette, which nearly landed him on the floor.

He caught his balance though and managed to gracefully bow towards his partner instead.

"Are you ready to be pummeled by this band of wild Amazons?"

He shook her head vehemently at her. "Not really. It seems to me that every group looks more ferocious than the last. I think you're raising up an army of wild women so you can overthrow the world."

"You're damn right I am, Ned, old boy. And you're just going to have to learn to live with it. And why is that, ladies?"

Suddenly the room came alive with the sound of a dozen empowered women's voices shouting in unison, "We're not going to take it any more!"

Officer Pearcy shouted back, like an army drill sergeant, "What was that? I can't hear you!"

Again the women shouted in unison, only this time even louder, "We're not going to take it any more!"

Officer Pearcy smiled at them then turned to Ned and shook her head, "God help you, you poor thing!"

To the women she said, "Okay ladies, line up. It's time to batter the batterer, to bully the bully, to beat the holy crap out of this guy. No holding back. Ned is well padded. Trust me. We've done this many times. He knows what he's up against, so let him have it with all you've got. Don't be taken in by that pretty face of his. Go get him!"

The women lined up at one end of the room. One at a time, they began to walk across the room. Each time Ned would approach them from the side or the back, and each time they let him have it with all their strength. They pummeled him with their fists, bit him, kicked him, elbowed him, and eventually he backed off. Some of them had mastered the more advanced techniques of kicking, blocking, chopping, and punching. While others who were less experienced resorted more to the old-fashioned cat fight techniques of biting and scratching.

I was very glad that I was not Ned, padding or no padding. These women were scary. They were powerful. The most amazing thing though was the amount of intense energy in the room. These were wild women. Women who were not to be messed with. You could feel their attitude. You could smell it in the air. It screamed, "We're not going to take it any more!"

While she watched the women beating on Ned, Officer Pearcy shouted words of encouragement to them. Some of the other women waiting in line did the same. It was truly an awesome experience to watch these women defend themselves against this huge man with bulging muscles. They were treating him as though he were an eighty-pound weakling. And while they fought him off one at a time, it was very clear that they worked emotionally as a group. The words of Helen Reddy's "I am Woman" song came back to me as though it were yesterday's hit. These women were roaring all right. It was impossible to ignore the incredible amount of psychological energy they generated. I felt stronger just watching and listening to them.

Officer Pearcy walked over to me, while she continued to shout words of support to the women. She paused in her shouting long enough to lean over and whisper in my ear, "So what do you think, Ms. Higgins?"

Her breath on my ear made the hair on my neck stand up. I smiled up at her. "This is great! I've never seen anything like it. I feel stronger just being here."

"Care to go a round with Mr. Tutu?"

"No thanks. I think I'll wait until I learn some of the moves first. I'd feel like a novice out there."

"Well, we're not here to impress anyone, but I do understand. Are you interested in coming back for the next round of classes?"

"Definitely!"

I had to shout to be heard over the cries of the Amazons in the heat of battle. One woman had actually knocked Ned off his feet. The whole group went crazy with applause and cheers.

"Whoa! I'd better go save Ned. Can you stick around after class tonight so I can give you all the information for the next session?"

I nodded my head as she walked over to make sure Ned was all right. He had already gotten up and was preparing himself for the next wild woman. When the last woman had her turn beating up the thug, Officer Pearcy began to talk again. She encouraged the women to continue with their self-defense education. She gave out a list of places that offered martial arts classes and informed them that there was a new one scheduled to open in the spring that would offer a woman-only class taught by a woman instructor. Its focus would be similar to this one, though it would concentrate more on perfecting the actual techniques of self-defense fighting.

She presented each woman with a certificate of completion for the course then invited everyone to stay for punch and cookies by way of celebration of their empowerment. Then she closed the session by yelling, "What's our motto?"

The Amazons shouted back, "We're not going to take it any more!"

"What was that?" Ned yelled.

"We're not going to take it any more!"

Ned yelled again. "Hey, I'm a man. I'm rather deaf sometimes. What was that you said?"

"We're not going to take it any more!" They thundered in returned.

Maybe it was the chill of my still damp clothes, or maybe it was the amount of womanpower in the room, but I suddenly got a bad case of goose bumps. As the exchange continued, I found myself yelling at the top of my lungs, "We're not going to take it any more!" And I meant it. No more, Ms. Nice Gal. I wasn't going to be afraid of Hardwick or any other two-bit thug on the street.

As the session wound down, Officer Pearcy was swamped by women wanting to express their gratitude for the class. Each of the women also thanked Ned; some of them even went so far as to hug him.

As I watched, I saw him bite down on his bottom lip. He was trying hard not to cry. I stood there in awe as I watched this big burly policeman wipe tears from his eyes. I marveled at the power of human beings to heal one another by allowing themselves to express their emotions

Here was a rough and tough policeman who looked, walked, and acted like a linebacker with tears streaming down his face. More than one woman came back a second time to hug him. Then Officer Pearcy walked over and gave him a big bear hug. She had tears in her eyes too.

Then all the women began hugging each other. I was engulfed in the mass hug session, even though I hadn't been part of this group. No one was going to be allowed to feel alone tonight. No doubt about it, the emotions in that room were powerful herbs of healing. Women who had been victims of violent crimes were finding healing in each other's arms and in the arms of those who had sworn "to serve and protect" them.

Chapter Fourteen

Refreshments were served at a couple tables that had been set up on one side of the room. The energy from the final session lingered in the air. You could actually feel the tingling sensation of the power of group dynamics.

I didn't really get a chance to talk to Officer Pearcy about the next session because there was always someone waiting to chat with her privately for a few moments. She bore all of this attention with patience and grace. For being such a tough looking female cop, she certainly seemed to be a very compassionate person.

After awhile, the women in the group started filing out in groups of twos and threes. One of the principles of self-protection for this group was to avoid walking in dark parking lots alone. A lesson I had learned the hard way. Perhaps it was the lateness of the hour; perhaps it was the sparkling conversation with Terri Jackson, but for whatever reason, I had not taken seriously the possibility that I might be endangering myself by walking out to my car alone before dawn. Looking back I realized that the hospital security personnel could have escorted me. I knew that I would have to rethink some of my habits, habits I'd taken for granted as being relatively safe.

As the last woman left the building, Ned began rolling up mats, while Officer Pearcy cleaned up the leftover debris from the celebration. She slid a huge trashcan over to the table and began throwing garbage into it.

She looked over at me. "I'll be done in just a

minute. Do you mind waiting? I'll walk you to your vehicle."

"No, I don't mind. I can help if you like."

"I never turn down an offer for assistance." She smiled at me as I walked over to the table and began clearing it of empty cups and half-eaten cookies.

"So, what'd you think?" Officer Pearcy looked at me with expectation in her eyes. She looked just a little like a child on Christmas morning. She was clearly proud of her work with these women and rightly so.

"I, well, I thought it was wonderful! Very inspiring. Not too mention empowering. By the time the class was over, I felt as though we could conquer the world."

"Yeah, ain't it great!" Officer Pearcy's eyes danced with delight. "I always look forward to the last session. It's always like this, and Ned and I bawl like a couple of babies every time. We just can't help ourselves. You should've seen these women when they first started. Some of them were rape victims, some muggings, and some that just heard about it from friends and were interested. But none of them vaguely resembled the group of powerful women you met tonight. These women are powerful warriors, gone out to claim their rightful place in this world."

"Do you ever see them after the classes end?"

"Sometimes. We maintain an open invitation for any graduates of the program. They can come to any future session without prior notice. Occasionally we get almost a reunion-like feeling going when several alumni show up at once."

"You and Ned are amazing. What you're doing here is great. I can't wait for the next session to start."

Officer Pearcy's face lit up. "So you're going to come?"

"Are you kidding? I wouldn't miss it. How do I sign up?"

"Registration is on the first night. I usually just tell everyone to come around 6:30, so we have a little time to get prepared for whatever group size we end up with. That way anyone can join at the last minute. There's a $25 fee that covers our cost for supplies and the room rental."

"Is there a class size limit?"

"No, we've never had more than 20 show up at once. Usually there are between twelve and fifteen women."

"And it's women-only?"

"Yes, except for Ned, of course. We have to have someone to beat on." She grinned and looked over her shoulder in Ned's direction. He had finished with the mats and was walking over to us.

"So, ladies, shall I escort the two of you to your vehicles?"

"Can it, you big lug. I'll see Ms. Higgins to her car."

"Well, I guess I've been put in my place yet again. You'd better watch it, Gerry, or I'm going get a complex from hanging out with you."

"Yeah, right. I am so believing that one, muscle boy. See you tomorrow."

"You got it." He bowed slightly in my direction. "Good evening, Ms. Higgins. I'm Ned."

I shook his extended hand, which dwarfed mine. "Yes, I know. You and Officer Pearcy apprehended a man who had been stalking me."

Ned looked thoughtful for a moment. "Oh yeah, Hardwick, the criminal wannabe. That guy's gonna do some serious time one of these days. For your sake, I hope he does it now, so you can have some peace of mind. Not much hope of that though, I hate to say it."

"So Officer Pearcy has told me."

"Well, I'll leave you women to it then. I've gotta go. The night is young, and my pool cue awaits."

Officer Pearcy smacked him on the back. "Later, hot shot. Win a few for me."

"Count on it."

Ned walked out of the room with his characteristic tough guy gait.

Officer Pearcy finished wiping up the table and pulled the plastic bag out of the garbage can. "Now if you'll excuse me. I have to throw this in the dumpster. Then I can fill you in completely on the class. Perhaps you'd like to go get a cup of coffee?"

"Sure, but shouldn't I go with you? You know, don't go out in the dark without a partner?"

"Oh, I'll have a partner, all right." She walked out into the hallway. She opened one of the lockers, pulled out her gun and holster, and strapped it around her ample waist. She patted the shiny black gun lovingly and said, "Meet my other partner. This one rarely leaves my side."

I nodded in understanding, only slightly intimidated by the presence of the policewoman's gun.

"I'll wait for you here then."

"I won't be more than a minute. The dumpster is right outside."

She disappeared around the corner, and I heard the creaking of a rusty hinge then a slamming door. Before I could even wonder how long she'd be gone, she was back.

"Okay, Ms. Higgins, let's blow this popsicle stand."

"Please, Officer Pearcy, call me Liz."

"Works for me. As long as you call me Gerry."

I smiled at her. "Sounds fair enough, Gerry. Officer Pearcy is a bit much to wrap my lips around."

Gerry smiled and looked as if she were about to say something, but thought better of it. Then she held out her elbow to me as though she wished to escort me in a literal sense. I reached up and slid my hand inside the crook of her arm and strode out of the room with her. Striding is the only way to explain how Gerry walked. She had that powerful demeanor of every police officer I've ever encountered. They must teach them how to walk and hold themselves when they go to the police academy. I wondered what it would be like to feel that strong and powerful. I've never seen myself as a wimp, but I've never had that much self-confidence. Gerry, on the other hand, oozed self-confidence and strength. I felt very safe as we walked through the dark parking lot to my car.

"Shall we sit in the car with the doors locked while we decide where to get coffee? That's one of my rules. Don't hang around in a parking lot. If you have to wait, do it in the car with the doors locked."

"Another good habit. I can see I've got a lot to learn about unsafe practices. I would've just stood outside talking to you. Though I have to admit that I feel very safe with you and your partner around."

"Ned or Missy?"

"Your gun has a name?"

"Yeah. So does my pick-up. Her name is Loretta. I named her after Loretta Lynn."

"The country singer?"

"Yep. But I suppose you don't listen to country

music. I figure you're more the New Age type. Am I right?"

"Well, not exactly. I'm really more into modern jazz."

She nodded her head in approval. "That would've been my second guess."

I unlocked the doors to my Corolla and slipped inside. Gerry carefully lowered herself into the seat, being careful not to bang her head on the way down. Toyotas are not known for being spacious, and mine was certainly no exception. Gerry's large frame looked somewhat cramped in the passenger's seat.

"So where would you like to go, Liz? There's a Dunkin Doughnuts near here. They have great chocolate cream doughnuts." From the look of surprise on my face, she realized that was probably not what I'd had in mine. She added quickly, "But I've eaten way too many of those this week already, and you probably don't eat junk like that. Have any other ideas?"

"I'm not hungry, so it really doesn't matter. I ate just before class."

"Actually I did too, but I work up one hell of an appetite during those classes."

"I can imagine." I racked my brains trying to come up with a place to go with this obviously ravenous police officer. "What about CDB's?"

"Good choice. I could go for some pizza right now."

"It's settled then. I guess I'll meet you there."

"Okay. I'll follow you."

"You're not driving a patrol car, are you?"

"No, I'm off duty. My pick-up is sitting right over there. Wet and lonely, kind of like..." She cut off the rest of her sentence then exited the car as quickly as she could extricate herself from its hold on her.

I leaned over and looked up at her. "Let me guess, you were about to say, 'kind of like me.' Right?"

Gerry shook her head and laughed. "You caught me. I tried to get out of that one. Sometimes police humor can be pretty crude. You get used to hearing and making remarks like that. It gets to be second nature after awhile. I'm sorry."

I laughed too. "Hey, don't worry about it. It actually sounded like something I might say, if I were in the right mood."

Gerry smiled back. "Okay then. Loretta and I will follow you to CDB's for some audacious pizza. I'm getting hungry just thinking about it. Mind if I call ahead?"

"You have a phone with you?"

"Of course. I'm never more than a phone call away. Would you like me to order something for you?"

"No, I'll figure out what to drink once I get there. It will give the waitress something to do."

"Gotcha. Later."

Gerry walked over to a small red 4X4 pick-up truck, unlocked it, and climbed in. She fit much better in her vehicle than she did in mine. I started the Toyota, turned on the headlights, and then pulled out of the parking lot. I headed in the direction of CDB's, keeping an eye on Loretta's headlights in the rearview mirror. I knew Gerry wouldn't get lost, but I felt more than a little uncomfortable with a cop following me. Even though I knew she was off-duty, I made a point to drive more cautiously than I've ever driven in my life. I could imagine her laughing to herself over my paranoia, but I couldn't help it. I'd never hung out with a policewoman before, so I wasn't sure how I was supposed to behave.

On the way to the restaurant, I finally decided that I should just be myself. It wasn't as though Gerry would arrest me for being a lesbian. She already knew that much about me and didn't seem to care. By the time I pulled into the parking lot, I had relaxed a little and was determined to enjoy myself with this woman who seemed to want to be friends with me.

As we waited to be seated, I strained my neck looking to see if Melissa were anywhere around. I didn't think she worked this late during the week, but she was on Christmas break right now, so I thought she might be trying to make some extra money during the holidays.

After about ten minutes, the hostess seated us in the side room. The restaurant was lavishly decorated for the holidays, and the people in attendance seemed to be in a festive mood. Even though Christmas was still a week away, you could tell that several parties were there to celebrate the season.

Gerry poured over the menu, pondering what to put on her pizza. I looked at her, a little puzzled, and said, "Didn't you call in an order?"

"I tried to, but the line was busy."

I recognized the waitress who came up to take our drink order. "Hi, Diane. Is Melissa working tonight?"

"Oh, hi. Liz, right?"

After I nodded my head, she went on to explain that Melissa had been there earlier, but had already gotten off for the night. I ordered a non-alcoholic beer and looked over at Gerry who was still deep in thought.

"Would you like anything to drink, M'am?" The waitress tried to get Gerry's attention.

"Oh, sorry. I'll have a Diet Pepsi or Coke or whatever you have that's diet."

"I'm afraid our Diet Pepsi tank isn't working right now. How about Diet 7-UP?"

Gerry looked a little disappointed, but accepted the substitute with aplomb. Then she went back to studying the menu. After a few more seconds she said in a mock British accent, "By Jove, I think I've got it."

"Got what?" I asked, amused by her impersonation.

"What I want to put on my pizza, of course. This pizza building is serious business, y'know."

"So it seems. I have to admit that I never thought much about pizza until my little sister started working here."

Gerry's eyes got very large. "You have a sister who works at CDB's?"

I laughed, thinking how odd it was that this police officer would be impressed by someone who worked at a pizza parlor. "Yes, she was one of the women at my apartment the night you and Ned picked up Hardwick."

"Oh, the cute little blonde teenager, right?"

I groaned inside. "Yes, the cute little blonde teenager. That's my sister."

"I guessed right away, even before I took your statements. You two look a lot alike."

"That would make me the cute big blonde adult then, right?"

Gerry looked me in the eye with a quizzical expression on her face. "Did I just step in something stinky?"

"I'm sorry. It's me. A family thing. Really. Don't worry about it. You didn't do anything wrong. I've just been going through this thing lately with my sister."

"I see. Or really I don't, but that's okay. You don't have to explain. I'll just tactfully change the subject."

We sat there in silence waiting for the waitress and a change of subject, neither of which seem to be forthcoming. Finally Gerry said, "Obviously I'm not too good at changing the subject. The cop in me wants to interrogate you. Or maybe that's the gossip in me. I'm not sure which."

She paused in her speech long enough to pull a pen from her top pocket. Then she picked up her napkin, folded it in half, and acted as though she were about to take notes on it.   "Go ahead. Spill it, Higgins. Spare me no details. Are we talking a classic case of sibling rivalry or what? What does your sister do that makes you completely ape-shit?"

I laughed at her comic routine. I was about to tell her my tale of woes when another waitress arrived with her pen and pad, looking for a food order. I had to bite my bottom lip to keep from laughing out loud as I looked at the waitress, then at Gerry, and back again. They looked as though they were both ready for action, pens poised in mid-air.

Gerry suddenly realized it too, so she dropped the pen and napkin and snatched up her menu again. "Okay, I'm ravenous, so I hope you have lots of ink in that pen because you'll need it for this order."

The waitress gave her a half-smile that was probably meant to be polite and friendly, but came off as snide and disgusted. Gerry was looking down at the menu so she missed it, which was just as well.

"I'll start with a Caesar salad. I also want some garlic cheese toast. Then for my meal, I'll have a large pepperoni and anchovy pizza."

Gerry closed her menu and smiled at the waitress who was clearly ignoring her jovial countenance, since it interfered with her bad mood. She took Gerry's menu from her then looked at me as if to say, "And what do you want, bitch?"

"I'm fine, thanks. I don't need anything to eat."

I handed her my menu and bit my bottom lip again. As the waitress walked away, I looked back at Gerry, who was sliding down in the booth while holding her napkin in front of her face like she was trying to hide from someone.

"God, what is it with me tonight? I feel like I just stepped in it again. Was she in a funk or what?"

I laughed as I watched Gerry sit up and place her napkin back on the table. Then I reached over and patted her hand.

"It's not you, Gerry. I think we must all be premenstrual. I'm sorry if I made you feel uncomfortable earlier. I do have a bit of a thing going on with my sister. It's less sibling rivalry than it is sibling envy. Ever since my sister sprouted breasts, I've been envious of her flawless looks."

"Oh please, Liz. You have nothing to be envious about. You're every bit as good looking as your sister."

"Then why does everybody always comment on my sister's looks to me? I feel as though they're always implying 'We can see who got all the good looks in the family.' I don't mind them admiring my little sister. I just wish they wouldn't tell me about it all the time. I feel like the ugly duckling."

Embarrassed by my outburst, I bowed my head and studied the napkin in my lap for a moment. Gerry cleared her throat then reached over and raised my chin so she could look me in the eyes.

"I'm sorry if I touched a sensitive nerve, but I think you're missing something here. You told me last week on the phone that you were lesbian, right?"

When I nodded my head as much as I could with her hand positioned under my chin, she continued.

"Then tonight you mentioned that your sister had been in the apartment the night I took your statements regarding the Hardwick case, right?"

Again I nodded my head slightly.

"I said something about her being the cute little blonde teenager."

Another nod.

"Then I made a point of saying what a big family resemblance there was, right?"

A tiny nod.

"Didn't you get it, Liz? That was clumsy ol' Gerry's way of complimenting you. Maybe even coming on to you a bit in a shy and harmless sort of way."

I looked intently at her. "You mean?"

"Yes, I mean."

She picked up her napkin and held it up again in front of her face. Only this time she used it as a curtain to shield herself from the rest of the restaurant. Then she whispered, "I'm a dyke, Liz, and I've been cruising you."

I started giggling until I saw the hurt look in her eyes. She tried to hide it and put on her tough cop look, but she wasn't fast enough for me. I shook my head and said, "I'm sorry. I'm being dense. I didn't realize. I'm very flattered."

Gerry nodded her head. "I see. I'm very flattered, but no thanks."

I shook my head again. "No, that's not it. I'm very flattered. I just didn't realize. I've been an emotional basket case ever since the mugging, and I'm trying to pull myself out of it. In case you hadn't noticed, I'm not doing a very good job of it. I feel as though I've been in an emotional whirlwind ever since it happened. I've been on the verge of tears a lot. I feel very small and fragile, and I guess I've been using my sister as an excuse. The truth is, I think the mugging bothered me more than I care to admit, which is why I contacted you about the classes.

"Then to complicate matters, I met a woman, Dr. Terri Jackson, at the hospital just before I got mugged. We're kind of seeing one another. So, I'm not really free to see anyone. Or maybe I am. I mean we've made love a couple times, but it's not as though we're engaged or going steady or whatever the hell it is that lesbians do when we fuse ourselves into coupledom. I mean I really just met her."

"Whoa, hold on, Liz. It's okay if you're seeing someone already. And from personal experience, if you two have made love a couple of times, then you probably are fused together as a couple. But just in case you're not, I'll tell you what I'll do. I'm going to see you at the class in two weeks time anyway. In the meantime, I'm going to give you my phone number. Then if you would like to talk to me before that time, either professionally or socially, feel free to call. I'll give you my cell phone number so you don't have to go through dispatch. I have voice mail, so if I'm busy you can just leave a message. Obviously if it's urgent, just call the station, and they'll get the message to me quickly."

Gerry laid her hand on top of mine and looked sweetly into my eyes as she said all this. I nodded my head and tried to wrestle with this new revelation. I had been startled to discover that Officer Pearcy was a lesbian. It wasn't that she didn't look like a lesbian.

On the contrary, she looked and acted very much like a lesbian to the point of being stereotypical. But I had thought that was just the police training. I just figured that female police officers had to be every bit as rough and tough as their male counterparts, even if they preferred to wear lace and nail polish when they were off-duty.

Then I laughed to myself as I thought about everything I had observed about Gerry tonight, from her red pick-up truck named Loretta to the way she got rid of Ned tonight when he offered to walk me to my car. How could I have missed all that?

I looked at Gerry and shook my head, smiling as I did.

"What? What are you smiling at?"

"Oh, just me. I'm so dense sometimes. Usually I imagine that women are lesbians even when they aren't. I don't know what happened to my radar with you. It must be malfunctioning. How could I have missed the signals? They were all there. Loud and clear."

"It's the uniform. That throws people sometimes. For the heterosexual women on the police force, it means contending with people who think they're lesbians just because they are policewomen. For lesbians, it's a matter of other lesbians missing what would otherwise be unmistakable clues. Catch-22, no doubt about it."

Just then the food began to arrive, and I was suddenly ravenous myself. Without much coaxing from Gerry, I found myself digging into the salad and cheese bread she'd ordered. I left the pizza to her though, since I detest anchovies.

Chapter Fifteen

After we had finished devouring Gerry's dinner, we left a big tip for the tired waitress then paid the bill and headed out the door. Before we went our separate ways, I said, "Gerry, can we sit in your pick-up and talk for a minute?"

"Sure. I think I can clear some space on the front seat. I'm a bit of a slob when it comes to my truck. It's really more like a portable locker. My house is much neater."

"That's okay, I promise not to look at how messy Loretta is."

Gerry smiled at my calling her truck by name then led the way to where she had parked.

"This, by the way, is a very bad parking spot. You should never ever park in a spot like this at night, if you're unarmed or alone. You see those trees over there? Damn good place for someone to hide. They also block the streetlight quite effectively. It's way too dark back here."

"Why did you park here then?"

"There were only two spots available in the lot when we pulled in. You got the well-lighted one, for which I was thankful, so I took this one. Had I been unarmed, I would have gone to another restaurant to eat."

"Really?"

"Really! It's not worth it to risk your life or dignity for a pizza. Not even one as good as CDB's. Of course, I've had lots of self-defense training too, which makes me a little less vulnerable. But if the other guy has a gun or a knife, and the element of surprise, then I'm not much better off. I try to live by the rules I've set up with the women in the class. It's really important that all women learn to be street smart."

"I know that now. By the way, are you armed now? You don't have your holster on any more."

"Perhaps you don't see my gun, but it's here under my windbreaker." She opened her jacket far enough for me to catch a glimpse of her shoulder holster.

"You mean we spent all that time in there and I didn't even notice you had a gun on you?"

"Yeah. See how easy it is to conceal a weapon?"

Gerry unlocked the passenger side of the pick-up and quickly threw some running shoes, a pair of sweats, and an empty Diet Pepsi bottle into the back seat of her extended cab. Then she patted the seat. "Hop in!"

After I was settled in the seat, she shut and locked the door then went around to the other side. I could tell that she was very alert to her surroundings. She kept her eyes moving, as though she were constantly on watch. She opened her door and swung up into the cab of the truck in one smooth, swift motion. She locked her door too then put the key in the ignition and turned the accessory switch on so she could play the radio.

"What's your favorite station?"

"103.7, but we can listen to whatever you like."

"Well, this is the young country station, but I'm pretty eclectic. I'll listen to anything really."

"Young country is fine. I don't mind that. It's the older country and western stuff that I find too comical to enjoy."

"I'm with you there. Here's a question for you. What do you get when you play a country song backwards?"

"I haven't a clue."

In a thickly accented country twang, she answered, "You git yer dawg back. You git yer pick-up back. You git yer girl back."

I groaned. "That's terrible."

Gerry grinned at me, looking quite pleased with herself. "I thought you'd get a kick out of that."

We both got quiet for a moment. Gerry was the first one to speak again. "So I thought you wanted to talk. Or do you just loathe the idea of parting from me?" She flashed me a charming smile that made me feel like I was being picked up in a lesbian bar by a handsome stranger.

"Well, a little of both, I suppose."

"Ooh, score one for ol' Gerry! She doesn't want to say 'good-night' yet."

She grinned even bigger. She reminded me of a little kid again. Her tomboyish charm was irresistible.

"I wanted to give you my phone number. In case, you know, in case you would like to talk sometime."

"I would say that's not a good idea because I just might call you every day. But the truth is, I already have it because of the Hardwick case. Remember when you asked me to call you if I heard that he was getting out?" She patted her right breast pocket. "Keep it with me all the time."

"Yes, of course. How foolish of me to forget. It's just that I'm finding it increasingly difficult to equate you with the foreboding policewoman I met recently. You have a name now and a face to go with the husky voice on the other end of the telephone line."

"Is that 'husky' as in sexy?"

"Oh, definitely."

"Now you see. I thought that would've given it

away right there."

"What?"

"My voice!"

"There are heterosexual women who have deep voices too, you know."

"But you said 'husky.' That's different. That's a bedroom kind of voice, right?"

"Yeah, so?"

"So? I was using my bedroom voice on purpose when I was talking to you on the phone the other day."

"What were you trying to do, seduce me on the phone?"

"If possible, yes. I am human, and I knew you were lesbian before you told me."

"How?"

"We-ell, when I found out who you were, I called a friend of mine. She and I went to the arts and crafts festival at Lake Morton last year. I thought I recognized your name once your sister identified you in the hospital, but I called just to make sure. You're a high profile lesbian in this mostly invisible lesbian community. Please don't tell me that you don't realize how famous you are in our small circle of like-minded people."

"No, actually, I guess I hadn't realized."

"Shoot, yes. Word spreads like an all points bulletin around here when a new dyke comes to town or at least comes out of the closet. You're pretty public about your love of women."

"Are you out?"

"Sort of. Lesbians know about me, but not many other people."

"What about Ned?"

"Oh, shit yeah. Ned knows. It would be pretty

hard to hide it from someone I see day in and day out. But he's cool about it. I think he thinks it's sexy. Not that he thinks I'm sexy, just the general idea of two women having sex together. We know each other way too well to think the other is sexy."

"But isn't it, well, illegal?"

"Only if you really stretch a point with our sodomy laws. Or you're a lesbian who does anal sex. Sodomy laws usually apply to anal sex of any kind, though gay males are usually the only ones who get charged with it. But Florida isn't all that strict about it, at least not this part of the state. Some areas are more homophobic than others. We're close enough to Orlando and Tampa that most people either don't care or don't notice us. But even so, I don't announce it at the station. I think Ned's the only one there that knows for sure. Not that it matters a whole lot what anyone thinks. A lot of people, cops and otherwise, just assume that most female cops are lesbians anyway. If nobody denies or affirms it, they can think what they want to think; it's only conjecture. But we're getting away from the subject at hand. What was that you were saying about me calling you? Was that a personal or professional offer?"

Her smile was infectious. I grinned back at her, and she winked at me. My heart did a flip inside my shirt, but I said calmly, "Either."

She pursed her lips and looked very serious. "I see. Either."

Then Gerry reached over to change the radio station. "What was that station again?"

"No, leave it there. It's nice for a change of pace. Besides, I like this song. Isn't that Mary Chapin Carpenter?"

"Now there's a babe in blue jeans! She's one I'd

love to nominate for a woman most likely to be desired by lesbians."

"Is she lesbian?"

"Not that I know of, but a gal can wish, drool, and fantasize, can't she?"

"You're really funny, once you let down that tough cop routine."

"Oh, I am, am I? So which do you like best, the tough part or the funny part?"

"All of it, I think. God, this is awful! I've been without a lover for over a year, and now all the sudden I meet a doctor and a cop all in the space of a couple days."

Gerry suddenly looked rather somber. "Yeah, too bad the doctor got to you first. Jeez, I met you only a few hours later."

"Well, more like a day or two."

"No, only a matter of a couple hours. I took the call about the mugging. I was at your bedside when you were still a Jane Doe."

"That was you? Terri, that is, Dr. Jackson, told me there was a policewoman outside, but I didn't realize that was you. Oh wait a minute! Terri did say that you were the same one she'd talked to at the hospital. What a weird coincidence."

Gerry answered quietly, "Yeah, funny how fate works sometimes."

I leaned over towards my companion. Her mood had changed rather quickly. "Are you all right?"

She nodded. "I'm fine, just a little disappointed. I mean when I was talking to the three of you at your apartment, I didn't realize that you and the doctor were already so involved."

"We weren't. That happened later that night."

"Wow! You two moved rather fast. I guess I'm

going to have to get faster on the draw, if I'm going to keep up in this town."

"Well, I don't usually get involved with anyone that suddenly. I think the extenuating circumstances drew the two of us together more rapidly than would have normally happened."

"And me with my tongue left hanging out of my mouth."

I sat back in the seat and laughed at that mental image. "That's a picturesque way of putting it. You know, Terri and I don't really know each other all that well, and we've had some problems already with compatibility."

"Oh sure, throw Gerry a bone. Keep her hanging on." She smiled at me.

"I'm not saying there isn't an attraction there. I'm just saying that I don't know that it's really going to lead anywhere, you know, permanently."

"Okay, I get it. But first you better find out about that."

"Yeah, I guess."

"You don't sound very sure of yourself."

"I'm not sure about anything right now."

"Why is that?"

"Because earlier today I was making love with Terri Jackson, but now I'm sitting here with you."

"And?"

"What do you mean 'and?'"

"I mean finish that thought out loud. You're thinking so loud, I can almost hear it, but my hearing isn't quite good enough. I'm not one of those people into ESP, you know. I prefer ESPN myself."

I giggled. Then I giggled again because I sounded so much like Melissa.

She leaned towards me. "Yes. Ms. Higgins, would

you like to share that funny thought with the rest of the class?"

Then I burst out laughing at her comical schoolteacher routine. "You are so funny."

"Come on, I'm not that funny. I think you're trying to avoid answering my question. I mean, you lure me into my truck to tell me what? That I was a few lousy hours too late to become your paramour? That sucks, Liz. Now at least tell me what you're thinking."

"Or what?" I said stubbornly.

"Or I'll, um, I'll tickle you. Yeah, that's right! The old triple tickle torture treatment!" She leaned over like she was about to tickle me, but stopped when I squealed. "Hey, I was only kidding." She looked very concerned. "I hope I didn't scare you. My brother used to pull that on me when I was a kid. Worked every time too, I'm here to tell ya. I'd confess to damn near anything when he started tickling me. It didn't matter if it was true or not. When you think about it, it's probably a good method of interrogation." She wriggled her eyebrows up and down maniacally.

"Yeah, but if you'd confess to things you didn't do, how fair is that?"

She scrunched up her face as though she were seriously considering my objection. "Hm. There is that, of course. So are you going to tell me what you were thinking, or do I need to kick you out of the truck?"

"Boy, you sure don't let go easily, do you?"

"Nope. I'm like a bulldog with a bone. That's what makes me a good cop. I don't get sidetracked that easily. Focus on the issue at hand. None of that sleight of hand stuff is going to keep me from getting the answers I want. However, I will respect your right not to answer my question until you've had a chance to call an attorney."

"Oh god, there's that too!"

"There's what?"

"My brother is an attorney."

Gerry reached over and turned off the radio then settled back into her seat. "Okay, I'll bite. What does that have to do with anything? And mind you, I haven't forgotten about my question. I will ask it again, and if you are refusing to answer me then tell me so bluntly, and I'll let it go. Otherwise, I'll think you've merely forgotten the question, and that I will eventually get an answer out of you if I keep reminding you about it. Now tell me about your brother the attorney."

I related the story about my mother's disappearance and the recent phone call to James. Gerry listened intently while I dumped this whole family matter into her lap. When I was finished, she looked at me intently. "So, do you think you're a lesbian because you're searching for your long lost mother?"

I chuckled. "You know, my brother asked me that same question several years when I came out to him. He was the second one I came out to, after my sister, who found out accidentally by reading one of my love letters."

"What did you tell him?"

"I told him that I had no idea why I was lesbian, but considering the thoughts and fantasies I had as a pre-adolescent, even before mother disappeared, I probably would've been lesbian no matter what."

"Ah, well that settles it then."

"I suppose. How does anyone know why they turn out to be gay or bisexual or whatever?"

"Whatever? I kinda like the sounds of whatever."

I grinned at her. "You're incorrigible."

"Yes, I suppose I am. By the way, how do you 'accidentally' read someone's love letter?"

She borrowed a jacket of mine and was cleaning out the pockets before she gave it back. She found a folded up piece of paper in there, which she thought was something of hers. It was addressed to 'my darling,' so she thought her boyfriend *du jour* might have slipped it in when she wasn't looking. She started reading and got very confused. Anyway, she asked me about it, so I came out to her."

"I guess you're out to everybody because of your artwork."

"Yeah, pretty much. It would be hard to miss once you see that."

"I'd like to see more of your work sometime, if that is okay."

"You mean that you'd like to come to my place to see my etchings?"

Gerry smiled slyly. "Well, if that line works for you, it for damn sure works for me." We were both quiet for a few seconds. Finally Gerry said, "Well, I've done a whole lot of listening about Liz's life. Do I get a peek inside of Liz's head now? Or have you decided to plead the fifth?"

"Now you see, I have forgotten what the question was now."

"Well, it wasn't really a question. It was more like a thought that you started, but didn't finish aloud. Let me see if my police mind is working as well as it should be. Um, I believe you were saying something like, 'earlier today I was making love with Terri Jackson, and now I'm sitting here with you.' You, of course, would be me, if you follow my train of thought."

I giggled again. "Boy, you do have a good memory."

"Does that mean you're pleading the fifth? It's okay if you don't want to tell me what you were thinking. Just tell me that you choose not to answer, and I promise to drop it and never bring it up again."

"No, I'll tell you. I just need a moment to get the thoughts sorted out in my head. I guess what I meant was that it seemed rather odd that I would start out relishing a sexual encounter with one woman, only to find myself wishing I could be enjoying a similar type of encounter with another woman. There, is that plain enough for you?"

"Thank you for being honest with me. I'm very flattered that you would want to have sex with me."

"What makes you think I was referring to you?"

Gerry grinned at me, her face turning red. "Uh, you got me. Perhaps because you were with me at the time you were having said lascivious thoughts?"

"Circumstantial evidence, officer."

"Then if I leaned over there and kissed you, you wouldn't enjoy yourself? Is that what you're trying to say?"

"Oh, I wouldn't go so far as to say that." I smirked.

"Hmm."

"Hmm? Is that all you're going to say?"

"Mm hmm."

We were both quiet for a few moments. Gerry broke the silence first. "You know, the sexual tension is so tight in this cab, I bet'cha Mary Chapin Carpenter could twang out a tune on it."

I let out a very slow, deep breath then whispered, "Yes, I suspect she could."

"And what do you think we should do about it?"

"I don't know. Turn on the radio?"

"Uh huh. Well, that would be at least two of us that would be turned on then."

"Or three."

Gerry reached over and turned the radio on again. She started to change the station, but I reached out my hand to stop her. "Don't. Leave it there. It fits the moment." Before I remove my hand, I let it slide down to Gerry's wrist first. Then I lightly brushed the inside of her wrist with my middle finger. Gerry shuddered visibly.

"You know, Liz, I'd better take you to your car before I do something you may regret in the morning."

"I try to live without regrets, Gerry."

"Meaning?" She looked at me with a penetrating look.

"Meaning I'm a big girl, and I take responsibility for my actions."

"My heart is pounding inside my shirt, Liz. Can you see it from there? That's your fault, y'know."

"Oh really? Can I feel it? I definitely can't see it from over here."

Gerry reached over, grasped my hand, and placed it lightly over her left breast pocket. I could feel her heart pounding beneath my palm, but I couldn't resist raising the stakes in this little game.

"I can just barely tell with all those clothes between your heart and my hand."

Then I slid my hand between the buttons of her shirt and slipped it down into the cup of her bra. Her breast felt as though it were on fire. I could feel her intense stare even though I wasn't looking at her eyes. I began to maneuver my hand down into the cup until I found her nipple, rigid and waiting for me.

"Liz, you're making me crazy. You do know that, don't you?" Her breath was ragged.

"I certainly hope so."

"Please don't fuck with my heart. When I fall, I fall all the way. Don't do that to me unless you're going there with me. I don't want to be with someone and not know whether we're a couple or not."

I slid my hand back out slowly.

"I'm not playing with you, Gerry. I really want you, but I'm also confused."

"About Terri?"

"Yes, and about myself."

"Meaning?"

"How can I be so attracted to two women at once, and what am I going to do about it? You're both so different, and yet I find myself drawn to both of you at the same time."

"Okay, Liz, here's what we're going to do." Gerry sounded breathless and more than just a little bit panicky. "We're going to get out of the truck and walk over to your car. Then you're going to go to your home, and I'm going to go to mine. We can try to sort this out later." She didn't give me a chance to protest. She simply got out of the truck and shut the door. Then she took a deep breath and walked around to the passenger side and opened the door for me. "Really, Liz, this is your last chance. Time for you to go home."

Reluctantly I slid out of the cab and walked over to my car and unlocked the door. Gerry had shut the truck door and followed me over there. Before I got into my car, I turned to look at her. "Gerry . . ."

"Nope, not a word. This is too much like torture for me. Go home."

Before I did, I gave her a light kiss on the lips.

She groaned, so I kissed her again with a little more passion. "Oh, God, Liz. I'm on fire already as it is. Please don't do this to me, darlin.' I don't think Gerry's soft heart can take it. Go home, I beg you. I can't do this. I can't steal you away from Terri. That's not the kind of game I play."

"But I..."

She put her index finger up against my lips to stop me from talking. I opened my mouth slightly and slid my tongue along her finger then captured her whole finger in my mouth.

I could feel her reserve give way. Suddenly she reached out and pinned my arms to the roof of my car and kissed me with more passion that I've ever felt in my life. Then just as suddenly she stopped and turned me loose. She took two steps away from me as though she could no longer trust herself to be near me. "Go home, Liz, before your tear my heart to shreds."

I nodded and got into the car as quickly as I could. She waited until I was belted in, with headlights on, before she went back to her truck. I backed out and headed for home. The last thing I saw in my rearview mirror was Gerry leaning over the steering wheel with her head resting on her hands. I wondered what song was playing on the radio.

Chapter Sixteen

On the drive back home, I found myself switching the radio station over to the young country one. Then I laughed at myself and changed it back to the jazz station. I might be able to listen to that stuff when I'm with Gerry, but it somehow lost its appeal without her presence. My mind was whirling with thoughts about my family and this weird thing with Gerry and Terri. I was sorry my sister wasn't going to be at my house tonight, because I was sure confused and could stand to talk with someone on the outside of it all.

Instead of driving home, I found myself driving to my father's house. There were a few lights on, so I decided to see if Melissa was still awake. I knocked softly on the front door, trying not to wake anyone. The porch light came on. Then I heard the door being unlatched. Melissa's face peered out at me. "Liz? What are you doing here at this hour? Dad is already in bed asleep. That pain medication they gave him really knocks him out."

"That's okay. I came over to see you anyway. Can I come in?"

"Of course." Melissa ushered me into the foyer. "Do you want something to eat or drink?"

"Maybe a glass of water."

"You look kind of funny. Are you okay? Did you get scared being alone at your place?"

I laughed. "No, I haven't even been home this evening." I followed her into the kitchen and sat down at the table when she handed me a glass of tap water. I took a sip then set it aside, remembering too late how bad the water tasted on this side of town.

"God, this stuff has not gotten any better over the years, has it?"

Melissa smiled apologetically. "No, why do you think I drink Coke, milk, tea, anything except this sulfur water?"

I shook my head.

She sat down across from me and placed both of her hands palms down on the table. "So, Liz, what are you doing here at two o'clock in the morning?"

"I don't know where to start. Do you remember the policewoman who helped to arrest that Hardwick creep?"

"Yeah, she was the same woman who was at the hospital when you got knocked on the head."

"Yes, that's the one."

I went on to relate this evening's events as they unfolded, beginning with the self-defense class and ending with the goodnight kiss. Melissa listened intently to my tale, nodding appreciatively about the self-defense class. Her eyes started to widen when I told her that Officer Pearcy was as queer as I was and that she had admitted to being attracted to me. She nearly choked when I told her how close I came to going home with her.

"What about Terri, Liz?"

"I don't know. That's the problem. I'm attracted to Terri. She's really nice and intelligent. She's good in bed."

"Um, Liz, please don't tell me about that part."

I looked at my blushing sister and smiled. "No, I wasn't planning on it. Just a general statement. What I meant was that it's not as though I'm not attracted to Terri any more. It's just that I'm *really* attracted to Gerry. I'm more attracted to her than anyone else I've ever met. It's downright animal-like.

I could have had sex with her right there in her truck and not cared who saw us."

"Liz, please, I think this is too much information for your little sister. I'm still a virgin, you know."

"Really? I've wondered about." I nodded my head thoughtfully. "But you see my dilemma, don't you?"

"Well, yes, it's not exactly as though it's never happened before. Isn't that what extramarital affairs are all about?"

"Yeah, I guess. But I've never been in this situation before. I really like Terri, but I also want the chance to get to know Gerry better."

"You mean you'd really like to have sex with her."

"Well, yes, to put it bluntly."

"Because if you just wanted to get to know her, you could do that without any problems occurring with Terri. But because you want to go to bed with her, you don't feel like you can do that because of Terri. Is that it?"

"How can you sit there so coolly and analyze all this?"

"Easy, it's not my heart that between stretched between two opposite poles."

"Yes, well, that would help, I suppose."

"So, Liz, if I were to come to you and say that I really like Robert, and we've been together for awhile, but I just met this other guy who really interests me even more, what would you say to me?"

"Mm, probably that you should think seriously about the situation. Figure out whether getting to know this other guy was worth the possibility of losing Robert. If it is, then you should back off from your relationship with Robert and give yourself a chance to get to know Joe Blow."

"Nice choice of names. Now if I told you that I

think you should do the same thing, what would you think?"

"It is a little more complicated though since Terri and I have had sex."

"Yes, more complicated, but you haven't taken vows of monogamy, have you?"

"No, but you don't understand lesbians."

"So, enlighten me."

"We-ell, lesbians tend to pair up rather quickly, and although nothing is said about mating for life, there's this unwritten code that says that you don't go around sleeping with other women while you're sleeping with the first woman."

"Uh huh. So it's like you're married already after one night of sex?"

"Sometimes, yes, unless it's implicitly stated ahead of time or it's a bar situation where the assumption is clear that it's a one night stand, even if it ends up lasting for several months."

"Then you'd better think long and hard about what you're going to say to Terri. She's really nice, Liz. You can't just going dumping her like that."

"I know, I know. I don't want to dump her. But it's not like we professed our love for each other. Hell, I don't even know for sure when I'm going to see her again. She's got such an odd schedule."

Melissa smiled at me. "And you don't?"

"Okay, so I do too. Gerry probably does too, what with being a police officer and all."

Melissa shook her head at me.

"What?"

"Nothing. I'm just glad I'm not in your shoes."

"Well, thanks for nothing." I smiled at her when she patted my hand.

"And here I thought you were so together."

"At last the truth comes out. Your sister is a basket case."

"You're not a basket case, but you should definitely say something to Terri before things get any worse. She doesn't deserve to be treated badly."

"Yes, you're right. Only I don't have the slightest clue what I should say. 'Hi, Terri, I had a nice time in bed with you the other day, but I just want to be friends now.' That seems a bit shallow, doesn't it?"

"Is it is possible for you to have two lovers?"

"Oh, I don't know. I don't think so. I don't think Gerry would go for it. Terri might be okay with it, since she isn't available very often, but that seems a little callous. I just don't think I could handle the logistics of juggling all three of our schedules. That always leaves someone out in the cold at some point. Better just to make a clean break of it."

"Well, then I think you have answered your own question."

"I have?"

"Yes. You say it would be better just to break up. I assume you meant with Terri, since you haven't slept with Gerry yet. Jeez, did you have to wind up with two women whose names rhyme?"

I smiled at her jest. Then I moaned at the reality of the situation. "God, this is awful. I really have to choose between these two women, both of whom I like a lot. Just shoot me now and get it over with it. I don't think I can stand this any more." I put my head down on the table.

"Come on, Liz, you're not going to find the answer etched on the kitchen table in tiny print, so why don't I make up the bed in your old room? We can have yet another sleepover."

I nodded and silently padded along behind her to

my old bedroom. At least those four walls wouldn't be screaming out to remind me of my recent sexual encounters with Terri Jackson.

Melissa loaned me a T-shirt to sleep in, so I changed quickly then fell into bed in an exhausted heap. I slid into an unconscious state immediately. No Technicolor dreams tonight. No Dolby soundtracks. Just quiet, blissful, oblivious sleep.

The next morning I put on my somewhat rumpled clothing from the night before and headed into the den, where Melissa had set up a bed for our father. Melissa had made pancakes for the three of us, so I sat with both of them in the den chatting amicably about dad's health, the weather, anything that didn't have to do with our mother or my crazy sexual life.

After breakfast, I cleaned up the cooking mess, so Melissa could slip off to the grocery store for some food items Dad had requested in his groggy state of mind. I sincerely doubted that he'd remember asking for them, but she insisted on getting him anything he wanted. I finished cleaning our dishes and began to scrub down the stove and kitchen counter. It suddenly occurred to me that I was avoiding being alone in the room with my father.

When Melissa returned, I helped her put the dishes away then promised to call her later in the week to find out how things were going. She was going to stay home all day to help Dad. Robert was supposed to come over to keep her company after he got off work tonight. I finally left after saying a quick goodbye to my father. I gave Melissa a hug on the way out. "Thanks for letting me dump all that stuff on you last night. It helped just to talk about it."

"Good. I'm glad to know I could return the favor for a change. You've listened to my problems for a long time. It's about time I was able to be the listener instead of the talker."

We hugged and I headed out the door. I drove home slowly, taking back roads, rather than the main drags. I knew I was trying to avoid going to my apartment. I wasn't sure why, but I suspected it was because I didn't want to talk to Terri, and she had my home phone number. Finally I decided that I should just go home and take a shower at least. Then I could see if I could get some work done.

As soon as I walked in the door the phone rang. I realized that I still hadn't purchased an answering machine, so I made a mental note to do so today. Then I picked up the receiver.

"Hello?"

"Liz? Where have you been? Did you go to bed early last night? I tried to call you several times. I was worried that something had happened to you at the self defense class."

I waited while Terri caught her breath, and before she could start again, I managed to say, "Good morning, Terri."

"Morning, hell, it's twelve-thirty. Did you just get up? Are you all right?"

I laughed. "Of course, I'm all right, Terri. You sound awfully worried. I'm okay, really."

Terri sighed. "Well, good. I've been wondering what happened to you."

I hesitated. I didn't want to explain about Gerry on the telephone. That seemed so cruel. And yet I didn't know if I could look into those beautiful eyes of hers and tell her that I'd found someone else. It wasn't as though I felt that we were going steady or anything. It wasn't as though we'd made any promises to each other. It wasn't as though I even believed what I was saying to myself.

"I stayed at my father's house last night."

"Oh. Is he all right?"

"Yeah, he's fine. Stoned most of the time, but happy to be home, I think."

"Good, and you're all right?"

"Of course, why wouldn't I be?"

"I don't know. You just sound a little funny— distant, I guess."

"I was up really late last night."

"So how was the self defense class?"

"It was really great, Terri! You should've been there. Gerry and Ned were awesome."

"Who are Gerry and Ned?"

"Remember the two police officers who arrested Hardwick?"

"Yeah?"

"They're the ones who teach the class."

"Oh, great. So it was good?"

"God, was it ever! I've never felt so much raw womanpower in one place. I can't even begin to describe it."

"How long did it last?"

"Until about nine."

"Oh."

"I ended up talking to Gerry, Officer Pearcy, that is, for quite a while afterwards."

"Really?"

"She's a lesbian, Terri, can you believe it?"

"Of course I believe it. She certainly came off that way to me the first time I talked to her, right after the mugging."

"Now you see? I didn't pick up on that. I usually do, but I thought it was just the tough cop exterior."

I could tell that Terri wanted to know more, but I

didn't really feel that I was ready to venture further into the tempestuous waters. After a long silence, Terri said, "So are you going to start seeing Gerry now?"

"What?"

"Are you and Gerry planning on seeing each other again?"

"Well, yeah, the self defense class starts up again in two weeks. I definitely want to go through the whole program. It was so amazing. Those two are great."

"Mm hmm. That's good. I'm glad you found out about it. That should help you a lot."

"Yeah."

"Liz?"

"What?"

"Are you going to start seeing Gerry? As in dating her? I mean, because it's okay. I mean, you know, I'm not around a lot, so that would probably be good for you if you did."

"What are you saying, Terri?"

"Look, Liz, I'll just be blunt, okay? You sound as though you are purposefully trying to distance yourself from me. You met another lesbian, whom you've described as being 'great.' I don't know. It just seems to me that you're trying to let me down gently. Like you want to see her, but you feel obligated to me because we made love a couple times. Am I getting warm here?"

"Oh god, Terri, you're right. That is what I'm doing. I'm purposefully putting up a wall between us. I'm sorry. All right, yes, I'm attracted to Gerry. And yes, I do feel obligated in a way. I know we never made any promises to each other, but we did have a lot of fun in bed."

"Yes, we did. But a relationship requires more than that. Like being together. I'm not likely to be around a lot. That has been my problem ever since I moved to Lakeland, and even this may prove to be only a temporary stop along the way. So, really, it's probably for the best that you've found someone else to date. As you pointed out, we're really very different. That would probably cause problems down the line again. So, you know, don't worry about me because I'm all right. I hope you and Gerry will be very happy together."

"Terri?"

"Yes, Liz?"

"Gerry and I may not end up together. I barely know her."

"True, and you barely got to know me, and look where I ended up."

"Ouch!"

"Sorry. That did sound a little bitter, didn't it?"

"Yes, but I deserved it."

"No, you don't deserve it. We're adults here, Liz. I can take this for what it is—complete and utter rejection. But I hope we can still be friends. I do like you a whole lot, and you're the only person I know who keeps late hours."

"You were teasing about the complete and utter rejection, weren't you?"

"Yes, but only partly. I won't lie and say that this doesn't sting. But really, I suspect it will be the best thing all around. I don't really have time for a love life even now that I'm out of med school. Who knows? Maybe I never will."

"Yes, you will, Terri. Once you get settled down somewhere, you'll find someone."

"Ah, well, that makes it all better then. So I guess

this means I'll be seeing you around. Is it okay if I still call to chat in the middle of the night? That is, if you don't have someone...or maybe not."

"Yes, you can call me. I don't think my schedule is going to undergo any radical changes."

"Okay, then. See you around."

"Yeah. See you."

I hung up the phone and allowed myself the luxury of a few tears. I knew we hadn't exactly been a match made in heaven, and we hadn't been together long, but that didn't mean I didn't care about Terri. She had been a great lover and an interesting person. I hoped we really would be able to remain friends. Even if Gerry and I didn't get together, this was probably the right choice for Terri and me anyway.

Chapter Seventeen

I decided to shower before I did anything else. Once I'd accomplished that, I headed over to the mall to look for an answering machine. I didn't really know much about the things, other than that I found them annoying. I found a relatively inexpensive one at Sears. I headed home with my mechanical receptionist and read enough of the instruction booklet to get the contraption ready for a trial run. I called Melissa to tell her what had transpired between Terri and me. She sounded relieved, but also a little sad that Terri was not likely to become part of our family.

Then I solicited her help in trying out my answering machine. We both hung up, and I waited for her to call. After she left a silly message, I checked the machine to be sure it had really recorded her words. Then I called her back to thank her for her help. Dad got on the phone too and mumbled some garbled stuff about how grateful he was for his two girls. He thanked me for helping to take care of him while he was in the hospital. Finally I got Melissa back on the line.

"Let me know if you need a break from watching dad. I could come over for a little while and work on my sketching while I sit with him."

"Thanks. I think I'm okay for now. We took a stroll around the house today, and he sat up for a few moments to watch television. I'm hoping he'll be up more tomorrow. The doctors don't want him to lie around too much and sitting isn't very comfortable for him, but he needs to start getting up and doing things for himself. I'll have to go to work again Friday evening, so he'll be on his own then. You can decide whether you'd like to come over and check on him that night. Stan already volunteered to take a long lunch tomorrow and Friday to come over and check on him. I'll get a break then too."

"Okay, well, if I don't see you before then, I'll call Friday to see how he's doing."

"Sounds good. So are you going to go out with Gerry now?"

"I don't know. I haven't called her yet with the news that Terri and I have broken up, though that seems like a stupid way to put it, since we weren't officially a couple."

"True. You were together what, three days maybe?"

"Yeah."

"Wow! That seems weird. I feel as though I've gotten to know her pretty well in that short amount of time. I feel like I know her much better than any of your past lovers."

"Yeah, well, you're older now, so that makes sense. But I know what you mean about feeling as though you know her. She's pretty easy to get to know. Very laid back. She doesn't seem to hold back anything of herself."

"Did she sound really hurt?"

"Um, sort of, but not too bad. She's the one who brought it up. Anyway, she was trying hard not to take it too personally, but I know it hurt a little bit. It had to. I mean, I ended up crying after we got off the phone, so I can't imagine that she wasn't hurt at all because of it."

"Do you think she would think it was weird if I called her? You know, just to say 'hi' and to tell her how dad's doing?"

I smiled knowingly. "Actually, I think that would be a great idea. You two hit it off better than we did anyway. There's no reason why we can't all still be friends."

"Oh good. Well, I'm going to go now. I hear dad in there mumbling something about corn flakes. Later, Liz."

I hung up the phone and allowed myself to feel just the slightest twinge of jealously. *O fickle heart of mine, you don't deserve Terri or Gerry.*

I found Gerry's cell phone number in the pocket of the jeans I had worn last night. With a surge of excitement and trepidation, I dialed the number. When her voice answered the phone, I felt my insides getting all tangled up in knots. My tongue seemed to have gotten caught in the tangling as well, but I managed to stammer a greeting.

"Liz! Hi there."

"Do you have a minute?"

"Yes, I have just about one minute. I'm getting ready to go into court."

"Oh, gosh, I'm sorry."

"No, no, it's all right. I was hoping it was you. Not many people have my personal number."

"Well, I'm flattered."

"So what can I do for you?"

"I just wanted to tell you that I talked to Terri today."

"And?"

"And we sort of broke up, though we weren't really officially together."

"Hmm. I see. Is she okay?"

"Well, yes, she's not devastated, if that's what you mean. Like I said, we weren't really officially together."

"Yes, you said that. I just haven't been sure who it was you were trying to convince."

"So . . ."

"Are you wondering when you can see me again? At least I'm hoping that's why you're telling me this."

"Y-yes, that's why I called." I suddenly felt stupidly shy with this self-confident woman.

"Well, I have to work until about eight tonight. Would you like me to stop by your house afterwards?"

"Yes. No. I mean, let's meet on neutral ground somewhere."

She gave a low chuckle. "Ah, you don't want to see me in a place where you've recently had a tryst with another woman. Is that it?"

"Am I that transparent?"

"To me you are."

"Then I guess I'd better be careful what I think around you."

"Oh no, don't do that. I like that you're transparent. Then I know exactly what I'm getting."

"And that's good, I hope?"

"Oh, yes. Listen, I've got to go into the courtroom now. I can't wait to see you. How about we just meet at CDB's at 8:15. Will that work for you?"

"8:15 at CDB's. You got it."

"Good. Liz, I—"

"Yes?"

"Nothing. I gotta go."

"Oh no, you're not going to get off that lightly, not after the interrogation you put me through last night. What were you going to say?"

"I just wanted to say 'thank you,' but it seemed like a stupid thing to say."

"Thank you for what?"

"I don't know. For calling me. For being alive. I'm not sure what. Just thank you."

"Okay. Well, you're welcome then, for whatever it was I did. See you tonight."

"Count on it."

When I hung up the phone, I discovered that I was shaking with excitement. I glanced at the clock and groaned when I realized that I still had over five hours before I would see Gerry. I didn't know what it was about this woman that made me weak in the knees. No one had ever had quite that effect on me. I didn't know if I was going to be able to stand being away from her for that many hours.

I went to my bedroom to think about what I would wear tonight. I pulled out a clean pair of jeans, a navy button-down oxford, clean socks, and a clean pair of underwear. I got out my backpack and stuffed yet another pair of clean underwear and socks in the bag. Then I pulled out a clean T-shirt for tomorrow. I grabbed my toiletries travel bag and stuffed it in the backpack too. I didn't know whether I'd be coming home tonight or not, but I was sure hoping I wouldn't be.

As I looked around my bedroom, my eyes fell upon the sketch I'd done of Terri sleeping on the couch. I never did get around to finishing that nude sketch of her, but perhaps that was for the best. I could always finish it later from memory, if I wanted. I felt a twinge of regret as I closed the door of my heart to that chapter. It had been a brief chapter, and not altogether a comfortable one, but it had also been sweet. Terri had been kind and caring and brave when I needed her. I would not forget that. I desperately hoped that we would remain friends.

I decided to give my apartment a good cleaning,

just on the off chance that we ended up here instead of her place. I really didn't have a clue where she lived. She might have housemates. She could live with her mother. I really didn't know that much about her life. All I knew is that I wanted to be with her, even if it was for just one night of wild sex. Gerry, however, didn't seem like the kind of person to go in for one night stands. She seemed more like the settling down type, a scary thought in and of itself. I've always been more of a free spirit. I'd take a lover now and again. Sometimes the relationship lasted a week, sometimes a few years. But never had I felt like settling down with one woman for life.

By the time I'd finished polishing all the fixtures, vacuuming the carpets, and mopping the floors, I was dripping with sweat. I jumped in the shower again and let the water cascade down my body. It felt good to have worked so hard physically. It felt even better to wash away the sweat from that hard work. Maybe this was how Melissa felt after a long run. It was a very rewarding sensuous experience.

I was ready and dressed way too early, so I decided to get out of the house before I started scrubbing things again. I drove to Lake Hollingsworth to watch the geese and swans. When I got there, I was rewarded by the last remnants of the evening sunset. I sat on a bench beside the lake and allowed the beauty of the moment to fill me. I was so happy I was about to burst. I felt as though I were on the cusp of something momentous. I was hoping it was love, but I was afraid to dwell on the subject. Better just to let things take their course. Everything always looks so rosy in the beginning, though, oddly enough, not with Terri. I guess that was a relationship that just wasn't meant to be more than it was, a lovely moment in time.

After the sun went down, the air cooled enough for me to want to be inside my car. I got in and locked all the doors. I stared out at the lake until I noticed that the moon had come into visual range. I nodded in her direction and thanked her for blessing the evening with her presence. She responded by shining a brilliant swath of light across the lake. It was so tantalizing, I wanted to get out of my car and follow the magical moonlit path until I found whatever was waiting for me at the other end.

When it was finally time to head for the restaurant, I felt a prickling sensation run from the base of my skull all the way down to my toes. It raised the hair on my arms. I decided to put on a light jacket to ward off what was either some sort of weird premonition or a warning of wintry weather just around the corner.

I pulled into the parking lot of CDB's at 8:10. I didn't see Loretta anywhere, so I parked in as bright a parking spot as I could find. I made sure my doors were locked, and I just sat there waiting. Within minutes, I saw Gerry pull into a parking space in the rear parking lot. When she got out and put a jacket on, I spotted the shoulder holster and its customary inhabitant, Missy. It was going to take some adjusting to get used to a woman who packed a gun all the time. I had to giggle as I pictured her in the shower with it.

She was grinning widely when she strode up to my car. I unlocked the door and opened it. "Hi," I said rather shyly, nearly overwhelmed by her butchy presence.

"Hi, yourself." She looked me up and down thoroughly. "Liz, you look so good to me, and I'm really hungry right now."

I flushed from head to toe startled by her boldness, yet very pleased at the same time. "Um, does that mean we need to go inside, or did you have something else in mind?"

"Oh, I have lots of things in mind, but first things first. Let's go eat. I hope you don't mind, but I ordered some stuff ahead of time because I know how I am when I get off work. I didn't want to have to wait for long."

"No, that's fine. I understand completely."

"We got seated pretty quickly, since Gerry had already ordered food that was ready to be delivered to our table. Gerry had ordered another round of cheese bread, as well as an antipasto salad. I had my own Caesar salad and some of her bread. I even ventured to have a slice of her pizza, part of which was only cheese. I think she ordered it, thinking it might be a little more tempting than something with anchovies. I had to confess that it was really good. Much better than any of the chain pizza parlors I'd tried in the past.

After a feast and a somewhat sporadic conversation about the day's activities, we left the restaurant. I looked at Gerry, who was suddenly looking very uncomfortable. We both knew what we wanted to do, but neither of us seemed capable of bringing up the subject. I decided to play it safe.

"Would you like to sit in your truck cab and chat before we decide what's next on the agenda for this date?"

She nodded, looking very relieved. Once we were inside, she turned the radio on, and I slid over closer to her.

She looked at me and shook her head slowly.

Then she breathed out a loud sigh. "God, Liz, you sure know how to torture a woman. Do you have any idea how badly I want you?"

I nodded my head. "Shall I check to see if your heart is pounding as hard as it was last night?" I reached over to put my hand inside her shirt. My fingers found their way to her nipple.

Gerry groaned and squirmed in her seat. Then she grasped my hand lightly and pulled it out of her shirt. "Look, I'm so wet right now, I need either to go home and change my clothes or lose them for the night. Which is it? You don't have to marry me tonight or tomorrow even. I won't put any strings on you. Hell, you don't even have to respect me in the morning. I just need to know if I can have you tonight. Here and now."

"Here? And now?"

"Okay, so that's figurative. I can drive to your place, or we can go to mine."

"Let's go to yours. Where is it?"

"Not far. Just follow me. I'll drive you around to your car."

"Okay."

She quickly started the ignition and nearly stalled the truck before she could pull out of the parking space.

She looked at me sheepishly. "Sorry, I'm a little tense."

"I understand perfectly."

She parked behind my car then jumped out of her truck and ran around to help me out. I laughed inside as I realized that I liked being treated with such chivalrous care and concern. Terri would have fallen over to see me.

"See you in a few minutes, Gerry."

As I got in my car to follow Gerry, I thought long and hard about Terri. Several thoughts ran through my head before I could properly process any of them. I knew that we hadn't whispered those three little magic words, yet I still felt a little guilty going from being with her one day to being with Gerry a couple days later. I couldn't honestly say that I felt anything close to love for Terri. I definitely liked her a lot. I thought she was sexy and attractive, and yet I was also constantly on the defensive with her, and I still hadn't figured out why. Maybe being with Gerry would provide me with some answers. Maybe it wouldn't.

All I knew is that I wanted this woman, and I wanted her badly. I couldn't say for certain when it had happened, but something in me had been switched on by this woman, and I was finding it impossible to turn it off. I didn't want to turn it off. I could taste my desire for her, and I could feel her desire for me. Perhaps it was enough. As I pulled up to her house just beyond the southern edge of city limits, I realized that it would have to be enough for now. I wasn't going to back out at the last minute, leaving Gerry wanting and myself wondering.

As soon as I got out of the car, she held up her hands to stop me. "Wait! I'm going to open the garage. You can park your car inside. There's enough room for two." So I got back into my Toyota and waited as she opened the garage door. Then I pulled in the right side of the two-car garage and put it into park. She closed the doors behind us.

Chapter Eighteen

How can I describe the feelings I experienced as she closed the garage doors behind us? On one hand, it might have felt confining, as though I had just walked into a trap. Instead I found that it made me feel safe and secure, a feeling I luxuriated in after the last few days of vulnerability. I considered the possibility that I was attracted to Gerry because she was a cop, which is someone I equate with safety and security. I decided to leave that thought on the back burner for now. I didn't want to overanalyze the situation, thereby ruining it completely.

Gerry fumbled with her keys, as she tried to open the back door. I found this endearing. This woman wanted me so badly she could hardly function. My heart warmed to her even more as I watched her drop the keys and have to start all over again. She finally got them to cooperate with her fingers, and the door swung open.

"See, I really do live here. I know you thought I was breaking into someone else's house."

I smiled at her. "I was beginning to wonder."

I walked through the door, which she closed and locked behind me. I decided to move quickly before discomfort could take over again or before I lost my nerve. When she turned away from the door to look at me, I leaned over and kissed her softly on the lips. Then I kissed her again. In that moment, I discovered two things about her. First of all, I found out that kissing her hello was an entirely different experience than kissing her goodbye. Last night I had kissed her in a desperate attempt to tear myself away from her, and she had kissed me back in hungry despair. Now tonight, in her softer kisses, I learned a second secret about her—that she had down pillows for lips. My mouth sunk into a softness that felt bottomless.

During our kisses, I could feel Gerry's heart pounding beneath her shirt. As our lips finally separated, it took a moment for Gerry to get her bearings. She stood there in a daze then shook her head. "Wow! You don't mess around, do you?"

"Just trying to break the ice."

"What ice? I'm about to combust spontaneously. What next? Do I just throw you down on the floor here?"

I started laughing and she did too. She began to imitate a cave dyke, "Ugh, gotta find a woman. Drag her off by hair and fuck brains out."

I nearly fell on the floor laughing at her hysterical antics. It felt good to laugh. I had laughed too little in the past several days. It was healing. Then she literally swept me off my feet and carried me into the living room. She set me down on a fake bear rug in front of a big stone fireplace.

"Me fuck pretty woman here. Make big fire. Then fuck brains out."

We started laughing again. Gerry slid to the floor beside me. "God, Liz, you make me crazy! I've never wanted anyone the way I want you."

"Oh sure. I bet you say that to all your cave sweethearts."

"All one of them!"

I laid back and allowed my body to sink into the fake fur. Gerry leaned over me and made love to my lips again. She held her body somewhat rigidly as she did this, as though she didn't want to squish me with the weight of her body. I pulled her close to me.

"It's okay, Gerry, I won't break."

"Liz, I weigh nearly 200 pounds, girl. You just might break if I let go of myself."

"Try me."

Gently she lowered a little bit of her weight onto me. I could tell that most of it was still balanced just to the left of my body, resting on one knee. She looked at me with fire in her eyes and began to unbutton my shirt. She reached in with her hand and cupped my right breast.

"Ooh, no bra. That makes my job easier. Now it's my turn to feel your pounding heart, you little devil, you. I still cannot believe you did that to me, twice no less."

I just smiled at her. She gently kneaded my breast, teasing the nipple into erection. When she was satisfied with her handiwork, she finished unbuttoning my shirt. Then she went to work on the left nipple. She teased it with her soft tongue, going around and around, occasionally darting in for a direct hit. Then she wrapped her mouth around my entire breast, as though she wished to consume it in one swallow. I exhaled very slowly, aware of the heat spreading throughout my body.

"God I want you, Liz," she whispered in her husky voice.

"Here I am, Gerry," I managed to whisper back.

She slid her tongue all along my side, causing a wake of goose bumps to follow in her path. I fumbled with my jeans, wishing desperately to be freed from any barrier that stood between my body and hers. Gerry reached down, and expertly unbuttoned and unzipped them. I raised my hips so she could slide the intruding material out of the way. Then she began to slide my underwear down my hips. I lifted up again, and found that not only had she slipped them off in an instant, but also that her tongue had already found its target.

I writhed under her expert touch. I moaned and swayed and allowed myself to fall completely under her control. Gently she plunged her big strong fingers inside of me. Then out again. Then in, then out. All the while her tongue manipulated my clitoris with a skill that may have come from years of practice or from sheer animal instinct. I couldn't tell which, and I didn't care. Instead of the typical fumbling around trying to learn what I like, she showed me what I liked. She teased me to the edge of oblivion then drew me back. Then she gently pushed again, closer and closer, until finally I fell off the precipice and into the refreshing pool of her love.

As I swam back to the surface, she kissed my thighs and made me want more of her touches. I dove again for deeper waters, this time nearly drowning in my desire to go deeper into her passion. At the bottom of the pool, I found a treasure chest. I struggled to open the lid, but found myself in desperate need of oxygen. I exhaled slowly and rose again to the surface. Gerry showed no mercy though. She sent me plunging yet again. Down, down, down to the bottom of the clear pool. This time I managed to open the treasure chest. Inside was Gerry's heart. I cupped it in my hands and swam back towards the surface.

I moaned out loud, "Stop, Gerry. No more. I have your heart now."

She looked at me tenderly, if a little quizzically. Then she laid her downy lips on mine again and reminded me what it is I love about women's kisses. Her kiss was soft and caressing. Yet there was also a hint of prodding with it. It was as if her lips were saying to me, "I don't have your heart yet, Liz."

I unbuttoned her shirt and unhooked her bra. She tore them off and threw them aside. I motioned for her to lose the pants. Then I rolled her onto her back and laid my head on her soft full breast. I could hear the pounding of her heart in my ear. I kissed her neck and nibbled on her ears. She groaned seductively. I wanted to move slowly with her to heighten her pleasure. I ran my hands slowly over her soft flesh. Her body was a perfect balance of softness and strength. Her muscles were taut from the workouts she endured regularly. Yet her curves were soft and voluptuous. Her full breasts and hips beckoned me to touch and kiss them.

Then there were her thighs, rock hard quadriceps combined with the softest of pillows just below her pubic area. I caressed and kissed her body from her head to her toes. Then I rolled her over onto her stomach and stroked every square inch of her backside. I glided my hand up and down her legs, gently coaxing her to spread them for me. Then I slipped my fingers inside her wetness. She groaned and called out to me. As I explored the lay of the land, I discovered that she liked me to tease her clitoris with one hand, while I plunged the fingers of my other hand inside. She exploded more rapidly than I expected then sunk down into the furry rug.

When I tried to find her again, she opened up to me even more. I suddenly wished I had bigger hands. I plunged in my whole hand, and rocked back and forth with her until she ignited into flames, throwing off little sparks from her smoldering body. I slipped my knee in behind the hand that was inside her to provide a little extra pressure. She exploded again and begged for mercy. After writhing for a few moments, she settled with a big sigh into the rug.

"Come here," she rasped.

I crawled back up to where her head was resting, her face framed by fake fur.

"Hi, did you have fun?" I whispered in her ear. I noticed in the half-light that her face was wet, as though she were crying.

"Are you all right, Gerry? I didn't hurt you, did I?"

She shook her head.

"What is it? Why are you crying?"

"Liz, I've never had an orgasm before."

"Are you serious?"

She nodded.

"Well, how? What?"

"I thought I was a hopeless stone butch. I have always loved making love to women, but I've never been able to let go of myself so they could really make love to me. I've tried, but I only got more and more frustrated."

"I had no idea."

"I know. I would've told you, but you never gave me a chance."

"But you did have one, didn't you?"

"Not just one, but three or four, I'm not quite sure. I rather lost my place in there somewhere."

"Wow! I'm glad I didn't know. Otherwise, I might not have succeeded." I wrapped my arms around her luscious body. "Wow! That's...wow!"

"Thank you, Liz. That was such a gift."

"You're welcome, Gerry, but it was not just a gift from me, it was a gift to me from you. You are such a beautiful woman. Thank you for trusting me so much. That was... "

"I know, wow!"

We laughed and hugged each other. I realized how

comfortable I was lying here with this beautiful mound of womanly flesh. I had never been with a large woman before, so this was a real treat. Her body felt so soft and natural. Her proportions seemed so perfect as I thought about all the women I had seen without clothes. I sat up and looked her up and down.

"I hope you won't think this is rude of me, but can I draw you naked sometime?"

Gerry chuckled. "Well, I don't know about that. Why would you want to do that?"

"Because you're beautiful, and that's what I do for a living."

"I know. I've seen your work. But I've never seen you draw any big naked women."

"I've never had any model for me. It's okay if you're not interested. I don't mean to push you. I just think that you're exquisite."

Gerry smiled at me. "Exquisite?"

"Exquisite. Luscious. Delicious. Voluptuous. What more can I say?"

"I'll think about it."

"Fair enough."

"Okay, I've thought about it."

"That was quick."

"I'm a woman of action."

"I can see that. And your verdict?"

"My verdict is yes, you may draw me, as long as you don't draw my face. I'm rather well known in this town. I'd rather not be that well-known."

"It's a deal. Besides, I never put anyone on display without prior approval."

"Then okay. Now come here, you."

She pulled me down to lie beside her again. She kissed me softly on the lips. I brushed her hair away from her eyes. In a matter of minutes, we were sound asleep, wrapped in each other's arms.

Chapter Nineteen

I awoke some time later. It was too dark for me to see, so I nudged Gerry to ask her where the bathroom was located. She mumbled that it was down at the end of the hallway. As I stumbled around trying to untangle myself from the bear rug, I saw that Gerry had gotten up at some point during the night to get us a blanket.

I managed to negotiate the path to the bathroom. I switched on the light and blinked at my reflection in the mirror. I looked like I had just had a wild night of sex. My hair was all over the place. None of it where it should have been, but it was too mixed up for me to figure out how to put it right. So I just left it the way it was and hoped Gerry would find it endearing to wake up to, rather than frightening. Fortunately it wasn't quite to the Medusa state.

I blew my nose on a tissue, while I emptied my bladder. Then I surveyed the bathroom, via the mirror, while I washed my hands in the sink. I was too tired to be curious, so I let her keep all her medicine cabinet mysteries to herself for a little while longer. After a quick flip or two of wild hairs, I decided I was as presentable as I was going to get in the middle of this night. I switched off the light and stumbled back down the hallway.

I pulled back the blanket to crawl in, but paused first to survey Gerry's voluptuous body again. Then I crawled in and wrapped my arms around her thick waist. Her body was warm and soft. I fell back to sleep after a brief reminiscence of the evening's proceedings. With a twinge of guilt, I wondered if Terri had tried to call me.

When I awoke again, it was daylight. I realized that I was alone under the covers. Then I heard what sounded like a toilet flushing. Then a shower started. I got up and walked down the hallway to the bathroom. The door was slightly ajar, so I hoped it was okay for me to slip inside. Through the steamed up glass doors, I could see Gerry's delicious body moving around in the shower. I thought about sneaking up behind her and getting into the shower without warning her. Then I decided it wasn't a good idea to sneak up on someone who was trained in self-defense. I wasn't in the mood for a black eye. So I greeted her instead.

"Morning, sexy cavewoman."

She turned around to face me. "Well, hello, sleepy head. How did you sleep last night?"

"Great. Mind if I join you in there?"

"Come on in. The water's fine."

I slid one of the doors back and stepped in behind her. I leaned over and kissed her neck. "Hi, lover."

She turned around to face me and gave me one of her soft kisses. "Hi, yourself. What would you like for breakfast?"

"What are my choices?"

"Well, I usually just eat Cheerios for breakfast, but I do have some eggs and bread, if you're brave enough to let me cook for you."

"Cheerios are fine."

"Good, that's easy."

"Yeah, but then, so are you." I smiled lecherously at her.

"I majored in easy at the police academy."

"Hmm. I'm not sure I like the sound of that."

"Oh, but there wasn't any real life training or anything, of course."

"Yeah, right. I'm believing that."

I pressed my body against hers as I reached around her for the soap. I lathered up and began to use myself as sponge to wash her body. I rinsed off my hands then began groping around trying to find her sweet spot. She groaned loudly when I located it. I pressed her up against the shower wall and kissed her freshly washed body. She writhed in pleasure as I worked her body into a frenzied state. She came quickly then slumped against me.

"God, Liz, how is it you can do that to me so easily? I've been trying for fifteen years for that feeling."

"I guess I was just lucky to be here at the right time."

"No, darlin', it's more than that."

I looked at her with lustful eyes and explored her body for more sensitive areas. It seemed to me that nearly every area of her body was erogenous. I had to wonder if her former lovers had been neophytes. I certainly wasn't having any trouble making her come. When she came a second time, she looked at me and said, "Okay, I give. No more this morning or I won't be able to walk. My legs are already a little wobbly."

"Oh, all right, if you insist, but it's so much fun. You are such a hot woman!"

She kissed me passionately on the lips. "I'm not the only hot one in this shower, girlie."

She wrapped her arms around me and lifted me off my feet. She pinned me against the shower wall, so I just wrapped by legs around her and held on for dear life. She sent me into passionate convulsions twice, once with her hands, then again with her soft mouth. We slid down into the bathtub, and she went at it again. I finally had to pound on her back to get her to let me catch my breath. Our passion was like a raging fire that was burning out of control, and it felt wonderful.

All my previous love affairs had been so controlled and civilized. It felt wonderful to be with a wild woman who wasn't afraid to make me feel her power. My lovemaking with Terri had been sweet and technically good, but it lacked this animal level of attraction that I felt with Gerry. I really wanted this woman in my bed, and for the first time in my life, I wanted a woman to stay with me forever. I wanted to live with her, to share my whole life with her. I had never experienced this before.

I laughed as I thought about how quickly we had moved. I barely knew this woman, and here I was ready to move in with her or have her move in with me. This was a first for me. I had always been very careful to maintain my distance from my lovers. They could live in their place, and I would live in mine, and we would just go out or sleep together whenever it was convenient. This was messy, and that's how I wanted it to be. It felt right that it was so messy. I had lived too neatly before. Everything had always been so well contained. But after last night, I knew that I was finally part of a real honest-to-goodness couple, and that's the way I wanted it. No more neat and convenient sexual arrangements. I wanted a real relationship, the kind I'd heard about and read about happening to other lesbians.

I'd always seen myself as being like one of the Greek Goddesses of old. I was Artemis, the self-sufficient woman who lived with a band of nymphs, but who gave herself wholly to no one. Now I found myself feeling more like Aphrodite, all sexy and seductive. I even wanted to be more like Hera, only with a lesbian twist. I wanted my life to become fused with Gerry's life. I couldn't figure out what had come over me, and I decided I'd better try to keep it to myself, just in case it was just a passing fancy. No need to get Gerry's hopes up.

"Tell me you'll marry me, Liz, and I'll let you up."

"I'll marry you, Gerry. Right after that becomes legal in this state."

"Legal? Hell, who said anything about legal? Just marry me, babe, just marry me. I'm serious. I don't want to let you out of my sight."

"Okay."

"You mean you'll consider it?"

"Yes, I'll consider it. There, I've considered it. The answer is 'yes.'"

"What? No 'maybe we should take things a little slower?'"

"No."

"No 'I don't know if we're a couple?'"

"No."

"I see. Then in that case, I really don't want to let you up. I want to kidnap you and carry you off to Australia or somewhere."

"Australia? Why Australia?"

"I don't know. It just seemed like a long way away from everything here. I don't want to lose you, Liz. I just found you, dammit."

"You're not going to lose me, Gerry. Believe me, I want this as badly as you do. This is completely opposite of the way I do things, but I'm ready for the U-Haul."

"Really?"

"Really."

"Hunh."

We stood there looking at each other in

amazement. Then she pressed her body up against mine and plunged me into ecstasy one last time before she finally let me up. She had to help me out of the shower because my legs didn't want to hold me up.

I managed to stammer, "You country gals sure know to make love."

"Yeah, we ride our mares hard and put 'em away wet."

I nodded and snickered. "Aptly put."

Since Gerry had the day off, we stayed at her house all day, making love and sleeping. Occasionally we ravaged the refrigerator, but we always managed to end up making love even while we were eating. The day was one big blur of sex, sex, and more sex.

The next morning Gerry put on her uniform to go to work, but I managed to remove it again. She didn't complain too loudly, even though she discovered that she was going to have to change her underwear before she left. In the end, she decided to take a spare pair to work with her. She was afraid of what she would do to them if she had any time to think about me while she was gone.

After she was dressed the second time, we managed to keep our hands off each other long enough to eat a bowl of Cheerios. Then she insisted that she had to go to work immediately. She was going to be late as it was. I slid my hand inside her shirt again. She groaned and tore off all her clothes just long enough for us to make love to each other one last time. Then she got dressed again and walked out the door to the garage. I put on my wrinkled clothes from the day before and followed her into the garage.

"No more kisses, Liz. You'll make me all wet

again." Then she turned and looked at me with pleading eyes. "Please be here tonight when I get off work."

"I will if I can. I may have to stay with my father tonight."

She groaned. "Okay, maybe that's for the best. I may not be able to move by tonight anyway. My muscles are already sore. I can just imagine what shape I'll be in tonight. Goodbye, Liz. I know I shouldn't say this yet, but I love you, girlie."

I couldn't believe my ears, nor could I believe my tongue when it blurted out, "I love you too, Gerry."

She smiled then turned to get into her truck. Then she remembered that she needed to open the garage door first. I told her to get in the truck and went to open the door for her. I blew her a kiss as she and Loretta drove away. I walked back into the garage, shaking my head. I couldn't begin to process everything that had happened overnight here. My entire world had turned itself inside out. I dreaded calling my sister, but I knew that was exactly what I needed to do, since my father might not be ready to be on his own yet.

After she drove off, I realized that I didn't have the key to the garage, so I would have to leave it unlocked. Hopefully no one would test it. I'd have to remember to let her to know about that. I glanced around at the contents of the garage looking for expensive items that I might need to hide in the house. Other than the washer and dryer, there didn't seem to be anything of value. She had an old 10-speed road bike hanging on one wall, but it was chained up. All the cabinets were bolted as well. Finally convinced that everything should be all right, I locked her back door and headed for home.

Chapter Twenty

I paid more attention to the scenery on the way back to my apartment. It had been too dark to see much of anything the night I drove out here. It was a nice drive back to civilization. Gerry's house was located just far enough away from the city to be cozy, but still near enough to be convenient. She lived in a subdivision outside city limits. Her house was a brown ranch style with a huge stone fireplace. It looked pretty big from the outside. My guess was that it had three bedrooms, though I hadn't allowed myself the luxury of a complete tour. I wanted Gerry to reveal herself and her house at her own pace. She was a mystery I was willing to unravel slowly.

As I pulled into my apartment complex, I realized the gravity of what had occurred in the past two days. I had told Gerry that I loved her. With a capital "L." She had told me the same. In all my years as a lesbian, I had never been the kind to bring a U-haul on the second date. Hell, we managed to survive the first date, just barely, without the moving van. I was still in a daze about it all.

I unlocked the door to my apartment then locked it again behind me. I changed into some cleaner clothes and went to survey the refrigerator. In spite of the Cheerios, I was feeling ravenous. Our lovemaking had been pretty athletic, and I must've burned off a thousand extra calories in the last 36 hours.

I found some leftover pasta, so I poured spaghetti sauce over it then grated Romano cheese on top. I heated it in the microwave while I rummaged for bread to eat with it. I quickly buttered two slices of sourdough then sprinkled Italian seasonings and Romano on top. I tossed the bread in the microwave while I began devouring the pasta. The bread was ready in a matter of seconds, so I began inhaling that too. It was an adequate chaser for this morning's bowl of Cheerios.

While I was washing dishes the phone rang. It was Terri. After a few polite exchanges, Terri got quiet for a moment then said. "Did you stay over at her place last night?"

I exhaled slowly.

"I'll take that as a 'yes.'"

"I don't know what to say, Terri."

"You don't have to say anything, Liz. What we did, um, I mean, it's okay. I told you that I didn't have any expectations about us. Hell, I know it's hard to be in a relationship with someone who's married to her job, so don't worry about it. I didn't expect you to see only me. I, um, I, well, you know. Whatever."

Tears stung my eyes as I listened to her valiant attempt to be magnanimous. She was doing a great job, but I could still sense the hurt in her voice.

"I'm really sorry, Terri. I don't know what came over us. We just..."

"Stop, Liz! I really don't want to hear about it. Give me a call some time, if you ever want to get together again."

"Terri!"

"What?"

"What are you saying? So long and thanks?"

"I'm saying, Liz, that I don't want to interfere. If you want to see Gerry, that's fine. If it doesn't work out and you want to call me, that's fine too. I'll wait to hear from you though. I don't want to breathe down your back."

"So you're just going to disappear?"

"Only if you don't call me. I know we had the 'Dear Jane' talk, but you know that sometimes things don't work out. I was just wandering how it was going. Now I know, so I'll leave you alone."

"This is how it ends?"

"Who said anything about endings? I still want to be your friend, but I'm finding it harder than I thought to walk away from this."

"I'm sorry, Terri. I don't know what to say."

"I'm sorry too. I realize that sleeping with someone twice hardly constitutes a long-term relationship, but neither was I expecting you to . . ."

"Go a-whoring?"

"Is that what you call what you did?"

"No. It wasn't like that at all."

"Then why did you say that?"

"Because I figured that's what you were thinking."

Terri breathed deeply. "You know, Liz, maybe this is for the best. You seem to want to cast me in the role of the bad guy all the time. But for your information, I'm not the bad guy."

"Right, and I am?"

"That's not what I meant!" Terri was obviously angry and upset now, and I felt like a heel. "I tried calling you several times last night, just to chat, but you weren't home. I got a little worried when you weren't home all night long. I didn't know you two were going to move that fast, but I guess I should've known better. I almost called the police though."

"You didn't!"

"No, I didn't. I figured that you were an adult and could take care of yourself." We were both silent for a moment, lost in our thoughts. "I know that I don't have any hold over you. I just wish you would've given us a chance, Liz. I don't know if we could've overcome whatever it was that kept us at odds with each other. I don't know if I could've found a position around here. I don't know anything. Except that I do care about you. A lot. But I guess that's not enough. Have a nice life, Liz. I'll try to do the same. Maybe one day we can be friends."

"Terri, I'm s—"

The phone went dead in my hand.

"Goddammit!" I yelled loud enough for the neighbors to hear. Then I sat down and cried until I could cry no more. What an idiot I was! Here I had met this wonderful woman and had proceeded to undermine our relationship from the very beginning.

I got in the shower in an attempt to wash away my anger and my guilt. It didn't work. The same heel got out of the shower as the one who had gotten into it, only the one getting out was wetter. As I stood there naked in the bathroom, I wiped off the moisture on the mirror and stared disapprovingly at my puffy red eyes and my stringy wet hair. "You're an idiot, Elizabeth Higgins, there's no getting around it this time." I said to the unsympathetic face in the glass.

I opened the bathroom door to let the steam escape from the room. The fan was broken, so it was difficult to keep the humidity under control. There was a knock at the door, so I threw on my bathrobe and walked over to look through the peephole. It was Melissa, thank goodness. I was in no shape to see any else at the moment. As I opened the door, the phone began to ring, so I motioned for her to come in and dashed for the phone.

"Hi, so are you totally and completely sorry about the last two days?"

"Gerry! Of course not. I can't talk right now

though, so I'll call you back. Is that all right?"

"Sure! Is someone there?"

"Yes, my sister just showed up. I really need to go. Talk to you later though. Bye!"

My sister looked at me funny. "Was that Terri?"

"No, that was Gerry."

"You do travel in interesting circles, Liz. First you're hanging out with doctors then you're flirting with policewomen. What has been going on since I left you last?"

"You don't want to know."

"Sure I do. Just don't tell me any intimate details."

"Where do I begin?"

"How about just after I left the scene last. You and Terri were breaking up, and you and Gerry were going to go out."

"Right. Let me get dressed really quick, and I'll fill you in on the last 48 hours."

Melissa tossed her duffel bag of sweaty running clothes on the floor and plunked herself down on the couch to wait for the review of my bizarre soap opera style love life. I returned shortly, fully clothed, and began to tell her my story. When I was done, she looked at me intently as though she were studying me.

"Are you sure you're my sister?"

"I'm not sure of anything right now, but neither do I know who else I would be. Weird, huh? Have you ever known me to throw myself so completely into a relationship?"

"No, as a matter of fact, I haven't. Are you sure you're Elizabeth Higgins? Let's see some ID."

I laughed at her.

"You know, come to think of it. None of this

started happening until after I got conked on the head. Maybe it messed up my neural patterns or something weird like that. You have to admit that I have been acting strangely, somewhat out of character. Don't you agree?"

"Well..."

"Don't you?"

"I don't know, Liz. You definitely acted weird with Terri. I mean, she's a gorgeous woman, and I couldn't figure out what you had against her. She seemed really nice to me. On the other hand, if you're just not made for someone, then no matter how hard you to try, it's not going to work, right?"

"I suppose. I don't know."

"Or let's say you are meant to be with Gerry. And somehow you knew you were going to meet the love or your life soon, so you purposefully sabotaged your relationship with Terri."

"That doesn't make sense, Melissa. Why go to all the trouble of meeting Terri, only to dump her for Gerry? Why not just ignore Terri completely and go on to meet Gerry?"

"Terri and Gerry. That sounds like a cartoon show I used to watch."

"That was Tom and Jerry, but yes, it does sound kind of silly."

We started laughing wholeheartedly, as only sisters can. It felt good to be able to step back from the situation far enough to see the comical side of it.

"So I guess Gerry's pretty sexy, huh? I can't imagine a cop being sexy. I can't even remember what she looks like. I just remember being glad she was on our side. The big muscle-bound guy too. I'll bet he scares the hell out of the bad guys."

"That's what Gerry said. But do you know what?

He's a teddy bear inside."

"Oh, come on. You're kidding me, right?"

So I explained in greater detail about the self-defense class.

"Wow! That sounds really cool. Can I come to those classes with you? I get kind of worried sometimes when I'm running. I run by myself because I can never find anyone to run with me. Besides, seeing that big burly cop in a pink tutu is more than I can resist. I can't believe he does that!"

"I know. I haven't seen him in his outfit yet. The last night of class he gets to come in regular clothes."

"So what's Gerry like?"

"Well, she's kind of butchy."

"You will explain that, won't you?"

"Okay, if I can. I'm not sure I can. It's hard to articulate. She has what our society might call 'masculine' energy. Only I don't see it as being 'masculine' because she's very much a woman. But she's a strong, powerful woman. So I guess you can say that she has active energy, rather than passive energy. I'm not explaining this well. It really isn't easy to put into words. Especially to try to explain it to someone who is heterosexual."

"I thought you were trying to talk me into being lesbian."

"Silly, I can't talk you into being anything. Are you lesbian?"

Melissa flopped back on the couch and put her arm over her eyes. "I'm beginning to think so."

"Why is that?"

She sat up again, and faced me squarely. "You know how you were explaining your love life to me?"

"Yes?"

"Well, that seems really exciting to me, and..."

"And heterosexual love affairs don't?"

"I guess you've been there, huh?"

"You'd better believe it. God I remember the first time I saw two women kiss. I nearly went ballistic, it turned me on so much."

"When was that?"

"It was at a concert in Tampa. I was in high school at the time. I went with James. Well, he gave me a ride then told me to go off with the friend who had come with me. He had his girlfriend with him and didn't want me tagging along for understandable reasons."

"Most everyone seemed to be pretty stoned by the time it was over. My friend and I were supposed to meet James at the concession stand, so we walked over there during the last song to wait for him. While we were waiting, we watched all the people who were still lying on blankets making out. I don't know if my friend figured it out or not, but I noticed that one of the couples on the ground was made up of two women. It was rather dark, but I clearly saw one of the woman's breasts as the other one lifted up her shirt to touch her. Then they kissed each other so passionately, I thought I was going to have to get a fire extinguisher. It was very intense."

Melissa shuddered as though a chill had just run down her spine.

"Are you okay?"

She shrugged. "I guess. I just got goose bumps. I think your description was getting to me. That's the kind of thing that makes me wonder. I sure hope I like Gerry. I really liked Terri, and I think I'm going to miss her. She was fun."

"Are you interested in dating Terri?"

"Oh Liz, I thought we'd been through this already.

What would we have in common?"

"I don't know. It's just that you've been so attracted to her from the very beginning. Am I right?"

"Yeah, I guess, but still. She's like twenty-something. I'm only eighteen."

"Doesn't matter. You don't have to marry her. Just go out with her. See how you feel about going out with a woman."

"Where would we go?"

"I don't know. I don't even know if she'll do it. I just put a big hole in her heart. I don't know how long she takes to heal."

"You're being too weird now, Liz."

"I am, aren't I? I guess I just want everyone to be happy and in love."

She sat up and slapped her leg. "That's it! You remind me of a little Cupid shooting arrows at people."

"Enough said. I get the hint. I'll leave well enough alone."

We talked for a few more minutes about our father's state of health. We concluded that he was doing well enough to be left alone for several hours. I volunteered to swing by and check on him before I got busy again with my artwork. Not that I was altogether sure I was going to be able to leave Gerry alone long enough to get any work done. I decided to call her back to see how she was doing. I went to my bedroom to make the call, leaving Melissa to her own devices.

Chapter Twenty-one

I picked up the telephone receiver next to my bed. I was rather nervous. I wasn't sure what I would say to Gerry. I wasn't sure what I should do. I had already told her that I might not be available tonight because I was going to check on my father. Now that I wasn't needed to sit with him, I didn't know whether to let her know I was free or to give her some time alone. I decided to give her the choice.

I dialed her cell phone number and got her voice mail. I left a message then hung up the phone. I lay back on my bed and closed my eyes. Allowing my mind to drift off to sleep. My head was filled with images of Gerry and her passionate responses to my lovemaking the last two nights. I marveled that I had been able to bring her to climax when no one before me had been able to do so. My heart was full of warmth and desire when the telephone rang.

"Hello?"

"Liz?"

Gerry's warm voice filled my head with loving memories. "Yes."

"Hi. You called?"

"I did."

"Thank you."

"For what?"

"For calling me back. I was a little afraid you'd had second thoughts about us."

"Oh, I've had second thoughts about us all right, and thirds and fourths. In fact, I've been thinking about us quite a bit. How about you?"

"Are you kidding me? I can't get you out of my mind. Ned has been giving me a hard time about it too, let me tell you. He's worse than a bulldog with a bone."

"Tell him I said that he needs to behave himself, or I'll tell all his friends about his pink tutu."

"Good idea. That ought to shut him up."

"How much does he know?"

"He doesn't know anything specific. He just asked me how you were in bed, and I spewed my coffee all over the dashboard. What else was there to say? I haven't told him squat, but I think he likes that better. Then he can imagine all kinds of things about us. Not that he could be much wilder in his imagination than we were in real life. God, Liz, you were wonderful last night. I'm still in shock."

"Good. A little bit of shaking up will do you a world of good. Where are you anyway?"

"I'm in the squad car. Ned is questioning a woman about a car prowl. I told him I needed to make a phone call, so he's handling this by himself. Not that he needs my help anyway. Routine stuff. A car is broken into. We fill out a report on what was taken, and she never sees it again. It's a rare case that we are able to recover stuff like that. But not that you really care about all this police talk."

"I care about you, Gerry. This is your life. So yes, I do care about it. Besides it may help me do a little reality therapy in my own life. If I can learn to be more aware of potential dangers, then maybe I won't get conked on the head again."

"I'm really sorry you were victimized, Liz. But I am glad I got to meet you. I don't know how else I could have made that happen. I saw you from a distance once at the arts festival. I had been looking at your exhibit with my friend, Bonnie. You weren't there at the time, so I didn't get to meet you. She saw you later and pointed you out in a crowd of people. I couldn't see you very well though. That's why I had to call Bonnie when I filled out the report on your mugging. I was pretty certain it was you, but I thought I'd make sure."

"I can't believe you knew all along I was a lesbian, while I was completely oblivious to your overtures."

"Well, I wasn't trying to be too obvious. That's a good way to set yourself up for disappointment. I wanted to be just dykey enough to trigger your radar, but not so forward as to make you run away. I started wondering whether you and the doctor were together when I ran into her again at your apartment. When I was trying to get information out of her at the hospital, she didn't seem to know much about you. But when we went to pick up Hardwick, there she was in your apartment. It was a little confusing, let me tell you."

"Yes, I'm sure. Terri and I met just before I got hit on the head. We had gotten a cup of coffee together at the hospital and had chatted for a little while. Then I wound up in the emergency room. She was concerned about me, so she came over later to check up on me."

"My god, a doctor who not only makes house calls, but examines her patients for free. I'm going to have to keep my eye of her. That sounds kind of kinky."

There was a moment of silence. Then she said, "I'm kidding, Liz. I can just see the wheels spinning in your head. If you were here in person, you could see that I'm grinning like the Cheshire cat. It was a joke. You can go ahead and laugh now."

"I wasn't sure if you were serious."

"I know, but trust me, most of the time, I'm not

serious. I'm a pretty silly woman. I almost have to be to counteract the serious nature of my job. Hey, it looks like Ned's about to escape from the clutches of yet another boring investigation, so I should hang up soon. Are you still going over to your father's house tonight?"

"Yes, but only for a quick visit. Melissa said that he's getting around on his own much better now."

"Good, I'm glad to hear he's doing better. Would it be totally inappropriate for me to ask if I can I come over then, or do you need some space?"

"No, I'm okay. You can come over. When should I expect you?"

"How about right after I get off work? That's at eight again tonight."

"Sure. That would be great."

"See you."

"Good-bye, Gerry."

I hung up the phone and closed my eyes again. I replayed the conversation in my head and began wondering who Bonnie was and how she would know what I looked like. Just then there was a quiet knock at my bedroom door.

"Liz? Are you awake?"

"Sure, Melissa, come on in."

"So when are you going to see Gerry again? I would like to meet her. You know, like a person, not as a cop."

"She's coming over tonight, but not until after you've gone to work."

"Darn! When is she supposed to get here tonight?"

"Not until after eight."

"So are you free for a little while?"

"Sure. What's on your mind?"

"I just have lots of questions about lesbianism. I

mean I'm not really sure what I should do on a date. I mean I know what to do with guys, or mostly what not to do with guys, but I haven't a clue about girls. Who starts things going?"

"You mean like putting their arm around you and kissing you?"

"Exactly. I just don't know how to go about being a lesbian. I spend most of my time with Robert trying to keep him from removing my clothes."

"Should I have a talk with that young man?"

Melissa giggled at my protective gesture. "No, I don't want you to have a talk with him. I think I'm going to break up with him anyway. I'm tired of playing the game. I think I'd rather be dateless than to keep pretending that I'm heterosexual."

"You don't know anyone in your class who is gay?"

"Well, yeah, but they're all guys. I haven't a clue about any girls. How would I know?"

"Think carefully. Are there any girls in your classes who never wear dresses or make-up?"

"A couple, but does that mean they're lesbian?"

"Not exactly, but it's not a bad place to start. Trust me there are lots of lesbians who wear dresses and make-up. But you stand a chance of finding one faster if you look for someone who's more of a tomboy. Start thinking about that. Think about the ones in sports too. Are there any who have never had a boyfriend that you can recall?"

"Hmm. Okay. I'll go make a list. Then what?"

"That depends on who winds up on the list."

She nodded her head thoughtfully and walked out of the room, closing the door behind her. I smiled to myself as I began to reminisce about my coming out days. It had been a long, drawn out process. I'd had clues about myself for years, but it never really hit me until I met Kelly. She was the first one. I was going to Florida Southern at the time. I'd thought I was a confused youth, but she was even more confused. She'd been sleeping around with every woman on campus, even some who weren't even lesbians.

Kelly was the kind of lesbian who could make you want to be a lesbian, even if you weren't. She had this raw energy inside her that drew out the lust in everyone, men and women alike. She certainly opened my eyes to the feelings I had inside. Luckily I didn't stay with her long. It was quite apparent that she was a tornado in search of a mobile home park. I didn't want to be in that park when she finally touched down.

Last I heard she not only got herself kicked out of school, but also managed to bring a professor down with her. She had been seeing one of the psychology professors for counseling. Somehow she managed to find her way into bed with both the professor and her husband. It was quite a scandal. The professor was fired; Kelly was permanently expelled; and the professor's husband, a college official, shot himself in the head. Very messy affair. As far as I know, Kelly's still out there messing up people's lives, or as in my case, yanking them out of the closet.

That was years ago though. I was older and hopefully wiser now. Or was I? I had just traded in what might have turned into a perfectly good relationship with Terri for a night of unbridled passion with Gerry. Okay, so two nights of unbridled passion. Where could we possibly go from there? Would anything ever top the power and passion of our first couple days together? I had my doubts. I guess I would have to wait and see. I knew I had a long way to go towards getting to know Gerry, but before I could find my seat on that train of thought, there was another knock at my door.

"It's open!"

I was expecting Melissa to walk in with her list of school friends. What I got instead was Terri standing in my doorway.

"Terri!"

"At least you still recognize me. Mind if I come in?"

"Of course not! Sit down."

She carefully circumvented my bed and sat herself down beside my drawing desk. "I probably shouldn't have come over without calling. I was on my way home from the hospital when I said to myself, 'What the hell? I can at least go over and talk to her.' It's not like I have anyone else to talk to. Besides there's just something I have to know."

"What's that?"

"Do you feel anything for me at all? I mean, besides contempt."

"Contempt? Why contempt?"

"Admit it, Liz, you've purposefully set yourself at odds with me from the start of this relationship. Everything I said, you had to find fault with it. Everything I did and everything I stand for. You don't like my choice of profession; you don't like my car. You don't like the way I eat or the music I listen to. What did you like about me, Liz? Or was I just someone to play around with until someone else came along?"

I took a deep breath and tried to think about how I could explain the inexplicable. "I guess I did seem that bad. I don't know what it was. It wasn't you though. I know that. It was me. I don't know. I was wound so tightly."

"Does that mean you're not wound tightly any more?"

"I don't feel that way at the moment. But really, it wasn't you, Terri. Something about you caused me to react. But it was me reacting to you. Not you causing it. That sounds stupid, I suppose."

"It doesn't really make anything clearer."

"No, it doesn't. I'm sorry. I'm sorry about everything. I was, still am really, attracted to you, Terri. I don't know what happened that night with Gerry. I just went berserk or something. It was pure chemistry. I don't know if there's anything else to it. I may not even like the woman once I get to know her better, but I just couldn't help myself. I couldn't keep my hands off her."

"Please, Liz."

"I'm sorry. I shouldn't have said that to you. I guess all I'm saying is that what has happened has happened. That may be all there is to it. I don't know Gerry well enough to know if there will be anything beyond that. It was like I was someone else for two days. A totally different person. My god, Terri, I ate Cheerios for breakfast!"

Terri snickered in spite of herself. "Cheerios? The woman from the nutrition police? That's it, the Twinkie defense. Remember the guy who shot Harvey Milk? He claimed that eating Twinkies made him to do it."

I laughed too. "Nice try. Unfortunately the Cheerios came after the fact, rather than before."

Terri nodded her head then turned to look out the window at the blue sky. I could tell that she was trying not to cry. When she turned back towards me, she gave me a sad smile. "So we can still be friends, can't we? I mean, isn't that a prerequisite for lesbian friendship anyway? Fuck first, talk later."

"Somehow that seems a little out of character for you."

"What? That I want to be friends or my description of lesbian relationships?"

"The latter."

"I'm right though, aren't I? Don't we always seem to get to know each other just long enough to decide that we want to find out what the other is like in bed? Then we have a love relationship for a while. Some of them last, no doubt. But most seem to fizzle out eventually. Then after a big blowout, we're able to settle down into a long-lasting platonic friendship."

I had to admit that what she was saying fit the pattern of my love life so far. "The good relationships turn into friendships. Hopefully the really bad ones turn into learning experiences we recover from eventually."

"True. But, Liz, I don't want to have the big blowout. Or perhaps we already did have it, and it was only a small one because we hadn't been together long. I realized on the way home that I have no other friends. If I lose you as a lover that is painful enough, but to lose you as a friend... My god, Liz, I've suddenly lost my whole social life, a life I'd only recently acquired."

"I would love to skip the big breakup scene, Terri, and I would love for us to remain friends."

Terri turned to stare out the window again. "Maybe that's all we were meant to be. Perhaps the strain of trying to be lovers was too much for us. We had a lot of fights over nothing, and we had only just begun to get to know each other."

She paused for a moment then turned to look at me. "So what about Gerry? What is it about her that draws you to her?"

"I don't know, Terri, to tell you the truth. I just don't know. Something about her turned on all the right switches. I don't know what it was exactly. I just know that it wasn't anything you did wrong. It was just something inside me."

By this time, tears were rolling down both our faces. I got up and walked over to where Terri was sitting. I put my arms around her. "Forgive me for being too stupid to realize that what I needed from you was friendship. Becoming your lover, only to turn away so soon, was cruel."

"I forgive you, Liz."

I held her tightly to my bosom. Just then Melissa poked her head into the room. Terri and I both turned to look at her, tears in our eyes.

"For crying out loud! I thought for sure that I'd be safe this time. I'm sorry."

Terri stood up and started to leave. "No need to apologize, Melissa, I was just leaving."

I reached out and caught her by the hand. "Don't leave yet, Terri. Stay and have dinner with me and Melissa too, if she doesn't have to leave for work right away."

Melissa piped up. "Actually, I was going to see if you could give me a ride to work later tonight. I don't want to have to call Robert, and I know Dad's not feeling so great. That's why I had Robert drop me off here after our little talk."

Terri raised one eyebrow at her, "Let me guess. You broke up with Robert?"

"Yeah, sort of."

"What's that supposed to mean?" I asked.

"I told him that I didn't want to go out with him for awhile. I didn't make it sound permanent, but it really is."

"Ah, the old delicate dump. I know how that feels."

"Terri, please." I looked at her pleadingly.

"I'm sorry, Liz. That was a lame attempt at humor, but I guess it's too soon for that."

"Much. But, yes, Melissa, I will either give you a ride or let you borrow my car." I turned towards Terri. "Now how about staying for dinner? We could have pizza, if you want."

"Pizza? I thought you didn't like pizza." Terri looked at me accusingly.

Melissa and I looked at each other knowingly.

"Terri, I like pizza all right. I just don't usually eat it because I don't want to gain weight. But starting today, I no longer care. I can take up running with Melissa in order to stay trim. I'm tired of being so controlled with my life. I'm going to start doing what I want to do and to hell with the consequences!"

Terri and Melissa exchanged puzzled looks. Terri was the first to speak. "Oh my god! I don't believe that came out of your mouth. I can't wait to talk to this Gerry woman. She must be some kind of a miracle worker. What has she done to you that caused you to change your whole perspective on life?"

"I'm not sure what happened. I just know that something came over me a couple days ago and a change in my attitude about eating is just one of the consequences. I actually think it happened at the self-defense class. There was just something about being with a group of empowered women. It made me realize that I've had way too tight a grip on my life and my bodily appetites. The other night I loosened that grip."

I related my experience with the self-defense class to Terri. "When I was standing there with that group of women shouting, 'We're not going to take it any more!' I realized that there were a lot of things I wasn't going to take any more. Much more than just overt things like muggings and stalkers. I suddenly saw that my need to control everything that went into my mouth was tied to a society that was trying to make me feel as though I should look like a concentration camp survivor. For years I've put down magazines like *Glamour* and *Cosmopolitan*, yet I still subscribed to the belief that I should look like the women who grace their covers.

"Later, as I held Gerry's big, beautiful body in my arms, I saw how stupid it was to think that thin is the shape we should all have. Thin is the shape thin people should have. It's not the shape most of us were born with. For the first time in my life, I had absolutely no sense of shame regarding my own body. None. Zilch. Zero."

I stopped ranting and raving long enough to take in their looks of astonishment, before continuing. "Don't worry, you two, I don't plan on going on an eating binge. I just plan to let go of the iron grip I've had on my diet and my life. If I gain a little weight, so what? Hopefully I'll be enjoying myself more. You may not know this, Melissa, but part of the reason I've never wanted to run with you is that I didn't want people to compare our bodies as we went running by. Also, I didn't want to add the weight of muscles to my body. Muscle weighs more than fat. I didn't want to gain any weight, even healthy weight, because then I would weigh more than those stupid charts they designed to help us reach our 'ideal weight.' I sometimes wonder how many women have killed themselves over those damned things.

"Anyway, that's what happened to me. It wasn't Gerry exactly, and yet it was Gerry. She was the one who showed me that women don't have to swallow the ridiculous pills our society prescribes for us. She also showed me that muscles and womanly fat look absolutely beautiful on a woman's body."

I climbed down from my proverbial soapbox, slid it quietly under the bed, and turned to face my stunned audience.

Without missing more than a beat or two, Terri said, "Then on that note, let's go order pizza! I'm starving."

Chapter Twenty-two

After the pizza was ordered, the three of us sat down and continued to talk about the messages our society had been sending us. By the time the pizza deliveryman showed up, we were ready to conquer the world, slice by pizza slice. I wrote the guy a check then settled down to a serious pizza munch. A little before six o'clock, I got up to take Melissa to work, but Terri volunteered to take her for me. She was starting to wind down and wanted to head for bed soon. I decided to run over to my father's house to check on him. We all hugged at the front door then I locked the door behind us as we departed.

After a brief and uneventful visit with my father, I returned home and collapsed on the couch. I fell asleep without realizing it then awoke with a start when the phone rang.

"How's my girlie?" Gerry asked in a seductive voice.

"Hi! I'm fine. Where are you?"

"I'm taking a coffee break at the station. I have to finish up some paperwork, then I'll be right over if you still want some company."

"Yeah, sure. I've been looking forward to it all day."

"Then I'll see you in about twenty minutes. Bye!"

"Bye, Gerry."

I jumped up and started cleaning the mess from the pizza orgy. I was about to take the trash out to the dumpster when I realized how dark it had gotten while I was sleeping. I decided to wait until Gerry got here to take it out.

I went to look in the bathroom mirror to see how I looked. I brushed my hair and my teeth, then went in search of something sexy to put on in time for Gerry's arrival. My wardrobe didn't really contain anything along the sexy line, so I settled for a clean pair of jeans and a slate blue silk shirt. I left the top three buttons unbuttoned—one more than I do when I wear it in public.

I turned on the stereo and put on a collection of sexy jazz music, the kind that screams "Take me to bed!" and settled down to wait for my lover. I didn't have long to wait. She was there exactly twenty minutes after I hung up from talking to her on the phone. I looked through the peephole at the uniformed woman who was standing on my threshold. She looked so official in that uniform. I'd have to get that off her quickly before my mood shifted to something other than sexy and seductive. She gave me a thorough investigation with her eyes as I swung open the door for her.

"Ooh, Liz, you look even better than I remembered."

She wrapped her arms around me and gave me a big hug. Then she removed her gun holster and laid it carefully on the floor next to the couch. She asked if she could borrow my shower, so she could wash off the sweat from a hard day at work. I nodded then began unbuttoning her uniform. Before I could remove all her clothes, she slipped her hands inside my shirt and began to caress my breasts.

"God, I missed you today, Liz! I couldn't get you off my mind to save my life. I wanted so badly to quit my job, drive over here, and whisk you away. How about Hawaii? Ever been to Hawaii?"

"Nope."

"Care to go tonight?"

"Tonight?"

"Yeah, tonight. Or if that's too far to go on such short notice, how about coming over to my place with me for a dip in the hot tub?"

"You have a hot tub?"

"I have a hot tub. What do you say to a little seduction in the spa?"

"I'll get my bathing suit."

"Don't bother!"

"It's that private?"

"It's that private."

"How about a towel?"

"Got plenty of towels."

"Something to sleep in afterwards?" I gave her a coy smile.

She smirked. "Who's going to sleep?"

"Something to wear tomorrow then?"

"Only if you insist."

She unbuttoned my shirt and kissed my breasts until both nipples became hard and erect, the areolas wrinkling up like two tiny relief maps. My silk shirt slid noiselessly to the floor. Soon my blue jeans joined it as Gerry laid me down on the living room carpet and infused my body with the fragrance of her passion. She filled my every sense with her tender lovemaking. She was every bit as sexually powerful as she had been night before, and I soon exploded in sexual release.

I removed the rest of her clothes then searched frantically for the path that would take us further into paradise. I found her soft, wet, and willing to go down that road with me. She convulsed under my touch almost immediately. She groaned deeply then relaxed against my body. The weight of her body against mine was reassuring. I fell more deeply in love with her at that moment. After a moment's respite, I took her down that path again. I could tell that the animal energy of last night was transforming itself into a deeper, long lasting desire.

After she had rested for a moment, she got up on one knee and said, "I'll get a shower when we get to my place. Go get your stuff while I gather up all my loose molecules. I know they're around here somewhere. I think I can put enough of them back together long enough to get us over to my house."

I put my clothes back on then grabbed some clean underwear and a T-shirt, turned off the stereo, and pronounced myself ready to go.

"That was fast. I haven't even found all my molecules yet. Care to drive my pick-up, or are you as wasted as I am?"

"I'm fine. You worked all day. I haven't worked in a couple days, thanks to you."

"Uh oh. Sounds like I'm a bad influence on you."

"On the contrary, you're a very good influence on me."

"Good. Here are the keys. Where's my gun?"

She gathered up her belongings and got dressed enough for decency's sake before we headed out the door. I helped her into the cab of the truck then climbed into the driver's seat. It felt funny to be sitting so high above the road, but the truck handled well, and we managed to get to her place without mishap. She got out of the truck to open the garage door, as we pulled into the driveway. I pulled into the garage, which she then shut and locked behind me."

"I forgot to tell you that I had to leave that unlocked today."

"That's fine. I figured you would. I keep everything

locked up in here anyway, so it doesn't really matter."

I looked at Gerry as she stood there in her garage looking obviously at home. I suddenly felt a little shy, as though I were a newlywed bride coming home after the honeymoon. Here is where it would all begin. The getting to know each other part. I was a little afraid of what I would discover about this woman I had fallen for so completely. I knew I loved her, but would I like her?

She had been able to reconnect most of her scattered molecules on the drive over, so she was looking steadier on her feet. She unlocked the back door with a little more finesse than the first time we came home together. She held the door open and waited for me to enter. She stuck her face in my hair as I passed. She kissed my neck and growled like a hungry feline. I tried to reach around to squeeze her rear end, but managed only to get caught on her gun.

"Ow!"

"Are you okay?"

"Yes, but I think Missy just bit me."

"I guess I should've warned you about that. She can be very jealous. I'll have to give her a good cleaning tomorrow, so she doesn't feel too left out. But right now it's hot tub time! Here, let me help you out of those confining clothes of yours." She shut and locked the door behind us then turned back towards me.

I kissed her hard on the lips. Then I stepped back and said, "Let me use your restroom first."

"Okay. I'll go make sure the tub is warm enough. Maybe I should give you a tour of the house before we jump in. I don't think you saw more than a few rooms when you were here before."

I nodded then headed for the bathroom. Her house was pretty warm, so I slipped off my jeans and underwear before I went back to her. I left my shirt on, though with only a couple buttons keeping it barely closed. I didn't know what it was about Gerry, but I seemed to be staying in a constant state of readiness with her. Something inside of me wanted to be so alluring, so sexually irresistible, that Gerry wouldn't be able to keep her hands off me. I wanted to drown in the waters of our lust for each other.

When I walked back to the living room, Gerry had already changed out of her uniform into some running shorts and a T-shirt. She was standing with her back towards me.

"I'm ready for my tour." I said casually.

She turned around and took one look at me. "What am I going to do with you, girlie? You're going to turn me into one big puddle! Look at you standing there, all soft and sexy."

"That was my plan."

"What? Murder by lust?"

"Sound like a case you'd care to investigate, Officer?"

She nodded her head eagerly then began to walk towards me like an animal preparing to pounce on its prey. "Have I told you yet how sexy you are?"

"Not nearly enough."

I turned as though I were about to walk back down the hall. She took two quick steps towards me, grabbed me gently with her left arm, and began cross-examining me with her right hand. She wound my pubic hairs around her fingers then slowly, methodically, began searching for clues. She quickly found evidence of my passion for her, but instead of taking me right there in the hallway, she scooped me up in her arms and carried me off to her bedroom. She laid me down on her king size bed then turned me onto my side. She got in bed and held me from behind as she began again to investigate my body. I was just about to climax when she leaned over me. "Look into my eyes, Liz, I want to watch you come."

I opened my eyes and looked into hers. Then I fell, hard and fast, into her brown eyes. I gasped then I let myself go. Our two bodies were intertwined, but our souls were being fused into one. I shut my eyes.

"No, look at me."

I opened them again, and she took me down with her again. Down into the depths of both of our beings.

"Now I have your heart, Liz."

I closed my eyes and rolled onto my back. She kissed me softly. Then she kissed me again. She pulled off her T-shirt then laid her full soft breasts on my stomach. Then she placed one of those precious mounds of flesh between my legs. The intensity of the softness sent my body into sensory overload. She pressed her body hard against me, and I came again beneath the pressure of her.

As I regained my composure, I reached down to bring her face up close to mine. "I love you, Gerry. I don't know who you are, but I love you."

I pulled her shorts down over her hips. Her dark pubic triangle beckoned to me. "Come here so I can reach you better."

I reached between her legs as she balanced herself on all four limbs, straddling my body. I stumbled through the wet tangle of her hair and slid down the bank to the stream that was flowing from her body. Like a kid in the hot summer sun, I splashed and played in her river of desire. The river soon became a waterfall, so we plunged together over the edge and went crashing into waters below. Exhausted, we swam ashore and fell asleep in each other's arms.

I awoke about an hour later. Gerry had collapsed on top of me. I struggle to extricate myself from her sleeping form. She moaned and rolled over onto her back. She was so cute, lying there so totally oblivious to the world around her. I got up carefully and slipped off to the bathroom. Gerry opened her eyes when I came back into the room. She propped herself up on one arm.

"Hi, I'm Gerry, and I'm a Liz-oholic."

I smiled at her sleepy face. She looked so adorable, lying there with her hair in a whirl of curls and dipsy-doodles. I sat down on the edge of the bed.

"Hi, I'm Liz, and I'm a Gerry-oholic."

She made a face. "That sounds like some sort of hideous medicine."

I nodded at her. "It does, doesn't it?"

Gerry lay back on her back, totally at ease with her nudity. I marveled as I thought about the variety of shapes and sizes women come in. I was finding that I liked Gerry's form better than any I had ever seen before. In fact, I was finding that, in my mind, her shape was quickly becoming the ideal feminine form. She looked so healthy and robust. So sturdy and invincible. Then I realized that for the first time in my life, I didn't envy my lover's body, I simply adored it. I was pleased by its aesthetic qualities. She reminded me of an ancient Mother Earth Goddess.

I reached over to stroke her stomach. She took my hand in hers then brought it to her lips. "I love you, Liz."

I squeezed her hand then leaned over and kissed

her lightly on the brow. "And now for the more direct tour of the house? I really enjoyed the scenic route."

She got up slowly and made her way over to the door. "Y'know, I don't mind walking so much. It's just that it's so hard to do it when they keep tilting the house."

"I think you're drunk on love."

"Mm hmm. I told you I was a Liz-oholic." She faked a hiccup then beckoned with her arm for me to join her on a second tour of the house. "As you noticed, there is also a bathroom in the master bedroom. Complete with a large shower for those unexpected sex orgies. Over here is the walk-in closet. It's really more like a drive-in closet. If you ever decide to move in here with me, you can park your Toyota there if you like."

I thought she was kidding until I opened the door and looked in. It really was big enough for me to park my car in it.

"The only flaw in the design is that the light switch is on the outside of the closet. It ends up being behind the door when it's opened, so you have to remember to turn on the switch first then open the door. Don't ask me why it's like that. It was that way when I bought the place."

We walked back out into the hallway. She gestured to her right. "That bathroom we've already christened, so I won't take you in there lest we get sidetracked again. Over here is an empty room, just waiting to become your art studio, should you decide that you're as crazy about me as I am about you."

I glanced into the vacant room. "What were you going to do with this room?"

"Nothing. I had no purpose for it. It came with the house. No extra charge. This room, however, is my exercise room."

We had moved back up the hallway to a third bedroom.

"Note the weight bench, barbells, and rowing machine. Thus the name 'exercise room.' I thought about naming it the torture chamber, but since I actually like subjecting myself to these sadistic practices, I decided that would be a misnomer."

As we came to the end of the hallway, she gestured to the right. "The front door is there. You'll probably never see that, since I always come in through the garage. Mostly I just use the foyer to house some bookshelves and hanging plants."

"You've slept in the living room, sort of. You met Gretsky, the faux bear rug, though I never formally introduced you two. If you'll look closely at him, you'll see he's really nothing more than a huge, flattened teddy bear. No live animals were used in his making. He's totally synthetic, but I don't hold that against him.

You've seen the kitchen from more than one perspective. I personally liked the one I got when I had my way with you on the table before I left for work today. Now there's a memory that's permanently enshrined in my mental photo album. Then there's the screened-in porch, out through the sliding glass doors that are hiding behind curtain number one in the living room. And that concludes the tour. You'll have to wait for the outside tour tomorrow when it's daylight. Are you ready for the hot tub?"

"Very ready."

"Could you grab a couple bath sheets out of the linen closet in the hallway. I'm afraid I neglected to point it out during the tour. Y'know it really is hard to get good help these days."

I smiled at her and went to get the towels. "What's the temperature out there?"

"In the tub, it's a warm 103 degrees. On the thermometer on the porch, it's a chilly 55. But that won't matter once you get in the tub. Just make sure you keep your towel handy for when you get out. That's when it gets cold."

I wrapped one of the towels around me and walked outside carrying the other one tucked under my arm.

"Is your yard fenced in?"

"Yes, there's a privacy fence all the way around the property."

"That's good."

"Modest?"

"A little. I can tell you aren't though."

"Not in my own backyard. Let me help you out of that towel and into the tub."

She hung my towel on a hook that was within arm's reach of the hot tub. I climbed into the spa and immersed myself in its delicious warmth. The jets gently massaged my muscles. Gerry climbed into the tub and settled down next to me.

"Now here's the scoop on the jets. There are a couple of them that will you find very stimulating, if you position yourself just right."

"Thanks, but I think you've been quite stimulating enough."

"No, really. Just try it for a second. You don't have to go all the way with it." She winked at me conspiratorially. "This one right here will do you from behind, if you sit like this." She positioned her body so as to receive the full effect of the jet flow on her vulva. She moved quickly though and beckoned me to try it. It would have been quite pleasing if I hadn't already been worn out from our lovemaking.

"Very nice," I said, as I moved away from the jet's reach. "How did you manage to go so long without having an orgasm with all this stimulation available to you?"

She smirked. "Well, I guess it was a poor substitute for having a flesh and blood woman in my arms. I get very aroused making love to women. But I don't usually get all that aroused when they try to make love to me. At least not until I met you. Probably the closest I ever came to having an orgasm was in this tub. Had you been in here with me, I know it would have happened. Of course, I don't need the spa when you're around.

"I'm embarrassed to say this, but I guess I will anyway. I bought the spa upon the recommendation of a sex therapist. She thought it might help. Who knows? Maybe it did prepare me for you. I know it has loosened me up since I got it."

"Then I suppose I owe your spa and your therapist my deepest appreciation. I've certainly benefited from your 'treatments,' shall we say?"

"Well, here's another secret for you then."

"Yes?"

"I usually wear my cowboy hat when I'm in here. It's over there behind you."

I smiled at her and reached for her hat. I put it on my head first, but it was too big, so I put in on hers instead. She patted my hand. "Don't worry, I'll get you one of your own, if you'd like."

"No, I think I should find a different style for hot-tubbing. Perhaps a fedora."

"We'll have to go hat shopping some time."

As we sat in the spa turning into a couple of pink

prunes, we discussed everything from the feminist movement to our favorite artists. We talked about her work and mine. As the minutes turned into hours, and our skin began to separate from our bones, I discovered that I liked Gerry a lot. I found her perspective of the world quite intriguing. When we finally got out of the tub, I realized too late that my legs had turned to jelly. Gerry had to help me get out. She swaddled me in the bath sheet and practically carried me into the house.

"I guess I should have warned you about that. Your muscles can get so relaxed in there they forget how to hold you up. I usually try to move around some when I'm in there, just to remind them that they do have a function in my body other than filling in the space between my bones and skin. I probably shouldn't have let you stay in there so long. I lost track of time."

"Oh, I'm okay. I'm just a weakling. I've been thinking about taking up running. My sister usually runs by herself because she can't find anyone who will run with her. I probably won't be able to keep up with her, but at least I can run with her for a while then wait until she returns. That way I can at least be a safety net for her."

"Tell you what. If we can work out the time frame, what do you say I keep you both company on my bicycle. I don't ride much any more, so it would give me a good excuse to start again."

"Sure, that would be great as long as we don't run too slowly for you."

"Oh well, I can ride in laps or something. It would at least provide her with another escort. Where does she usually run?"

"I don't know exactly. She has several different

routes."

"Well, find out, and let's see if we can work out the details. I hate the thought of her running alone, especially if she runs after dark."

Chapter Twenty-three

The next two weeks passed quickly. When Gerry was on-duty, I worked on my art. When Gerry was off-duty, I worked on her. Terri and I were gradually finding our way around the awkwardness of having recently been lovers. We were settling somewhat comfortably into a friendship. She, of course, was at the hospital most of the time, but when she wasn't, she often came over to eat or just hang out with me while I worked on a sketch. I never did have her pose again for the sketch I'd started of her. I finished it on my own one night. It was a beautiful piece. I hoped she would let me exhibit it some day.

I started running with Melissa several times a week. I was pleasantly surprised at the changes it wrought in my body. I knew I would never be the long distance maniac Melissa was, but that was fine with me. We usually ran around Lake Hollingsworth near Florida Southern. It was three miles in circumference. I built up to where I could get around it once, with much huffing and puffing. Then Gerry would ride her bike while Melissa ran a second lap around it. On days when I didn't feel up to running, and Gerry was at work, I borrowed Gerry's bicycle and rode along beside my sister.

After a couple weeks of dating, Gerry and I began discussing my moving in with her. The drive back and forth between our separate abodes seemed ridiculous. I wasn't particularly attached to my apartment, and Gerry's house was big enough for both of us.

The final decision was reached when Gerry called

me from work one day to let me know that Hardwick would probably be released in two weeks. His total stint in jail would be only one month. He'd behaved like a perfect angel so far, and the jails were filling up with wife beaters. According to Gerry that happened frequently with the increased pressures of the holidays. Then with Super Bowl weekend drawing near, the county knew they needed to make room for more incoming offenders. Until I started hanging around with a police officer, I had no idea that wife battering increased so significantly during major sports events.

As for Hardwick, he would be on probation for a year. Plus the restraining order that required him to stay away from me would go in effect the moment he stepped foot outside of jail. Gerry promised to make sure that the paperwork was put through correctly and in a timely fashion. Moving in with Gerry seemed like an excellent way to provide me with additional protection. If Hardwick didn't know where I lived, he could hardly stalk me.

Moving day was set for one week before Hardwick was due to be released. Ned and Gerry had made a visit to the manager of my apartment complex. They convinced him that it would be wise to release me from my rental agreement. They agreed to add an extra patrol car for the first two weeks after his release, just in case he decided to show up at the apartment complex. They provided the management with copies of his mug shots, and encouraged them to call the police if he ever stepped foot on the property. Even though I would no longer live there, the restraining order was going to include my old address. My new address was not listed on the court order, but was included in the provision that he could not approach me at any time, in any location. There wasn't any sense in giving him my new address. Since the phone was listed in Gerry's name, he wouldn't be able to get my new phone number. Everything seemed to be in order.

When moving day arrived, Gerry, Ned, Terri, and Melissa came over to help me move. Dad wasn't allowed to lift anything heavy, so we ordered him to stay home. We didn't want him to be tempted to lend a hand and wind up in bed again with another back injury. We used Gerry's pick-up truck to load the furniture I was taking with me. I sold or gave away the rest of it. We brought over my old bed to use as a guest bed in the art studio. The rest of my belongings got packed into Ned's LTD, Terri's Pontiac, and my Toyota. It didn't take long to get everything transferred over. Ned and Gerry shuffled the heavy furniture around as though it were made for a dollhouse. Melissa, Terri, and I arranged and unloaded my other belongings.

Then Gerry drove off to pick up a case of beer and a stack of pizzas. While she was gone, we all sprawled out on the floor and discussed the merits of various self-defense tactics. We all agreed that pepper spray was fine, if the guy was already in your face. None of us women were particularly interested in packing a gun, but we decided that cell phones could be helpful in preventing trouble or for summoning help after the fact. Ned started evaluating different forms of self-defense tactics. He explained that some of them aren't particularly helpful once your opponent has you on the ground. Obviously avoiding a dangerous situation was the best form of self-defense, but he recommended judo and jui-jitsu as being the best schools to teach us what to do if we ever had to grapple with an opponent on the ground.

Another session of self-defense classes had started, and not only was I attending them, but so were Melissa and Terri. They had both been shaken up by my experience and thought that it might help them to avoid a similar encounter.

When Gerry entered, we were taking turns learning how to throw Ned to the ground. "Hey, now! Children! Can I not leave you alone for a moment? Where are your exercise mats and safety gear? Who's going to pay for the lamp when it gets knocked over and broken?" Gerry boomed in her authoritative voice, clapping her hands together a few times to get our attention.

Duly chastised, we stopped our lessons and fell to grappling with the pizza and beer instead. As we ate, Gerry started in on us again, "You know, Ned, I would at least expect you to know better than to start tumbling without the mats."

Ned looked at each one of us, and with an embarrassed look on his face he said, "Uh, well, actually I was the one who started it."

Gerry slapped him on the back and shook her head. "I should have known it was your idea, kindergarten cop. Any excuse to wrestle a woman to the floor. Sheesh. What am I going to do with you, my friend?"

After everyone went home, Gerry wrapped her strong arms around me and whispered huskily in my ear, "So how do you feel about being here? Are you okay with it?"

I smiled and nodded my head, thinking about how safe I felt and how loved.

"Because I want you to feel as though this is your

house too. I'd like to work up the legal documents so that your name is on the deed as an equal partner."

"But I'm not an equal partner. I just moved in."

"Liz, if it were legal for you to marry me, would you?"

"I think so, yes. I've never really thought about it, since it isn't really an option."

"Then consider us married. If it has my name on it, I want you to know that it's yours too."

"I appreciate that. But it really isn't necessary."

"It is for me. I love you, Liz. Forever. I told you that I fall hard, and I meant it. I knew you were the one for me from the first day I met you."

"Really?"

"Yeah, really. I just didn't know how to go about convincing you of that fact."

"Amazing."

"Yeah, it is. So when did you know I was the one for you?"

"When I found your heart in a treasure chest when you made love to me the first time."

"Oh. A treasure chest, huh? Hmm. I guess I missed that part."

"No, you were right there with me."

"Oh yes, of course, I remember now. A treasure chest, buried at the bottom of the sea, with lots of crusty barnacles on it."

"Well, actually, it was at the bottom of a clear pool. And it had no barnacles, only very rusty hinges."

"Of course. I was merely testing you."

"How'd I do?"

"The same as you always do, girlie. You excelled. Now shut up and kiss me before my lips go into withdrawal."

I did more than kiss her that night. We made love until early in the morning. It was a wonderful night and the beginning of a new life for me. I felt safe. I felt loved. I felt wanted. I had come home at last. No more roaming the forest with a band of nymphs. Artemis had finally found a place to call home.

Afterword
The Goddess Series

Artemisian Artist is the first book in a series by
Beth Mitchum. Each book in the series is dedicated
to a different Goddess. Forthcoming titles in the series are *Gaia's Guardian, Demeter's Daughter,* and
Hestia's Healer. Although the Goddesses represented
here are all Greek Goddesses, there is no connection
between the books and the land of Greece, except in
a metaphorical sense. The books are dedicated to the
spiritual energy these Goddesses can bring to our
lives by helping us to become all that we can be.

All the books in the series deal with the charac-
ters introduced in *Artemisian Artist.* The books that
will follow continue the thread of the story found in
the first book, each focusing on one of the four
women—Liz, Melissa, Terri, and Gerry. Together they
weave a tapestry of women's empowerment through
self growth and strong relationships.

Author Biography

Beth Mitchum was raised in central Florida. She attended college there then went to work in a children's home, where she cared for abused teens for over four years. She moved to western North Carolina in 1985, where she was able to pursue her love of nature and the outdoors. While there, she earned a Masters degree in humanities and now continues her studies on her own.

She has spent all her life engaging in creative endeavors. After teaching herself to play the guitar at age 12, she began writing songs. You can enjoy her creativity through music by purchasing *Driftwood: the Music*, a CD companion to her first novel, *Driftwood*.

Beth lives in western Washington with her two cats, Dustin and Bingo. When the cats allow her, Beth works on her website. You will find it at www.ultravioletlove.com. The website is dedicated to "making lesbian love visible," by promoting the work and play of lesbians in cyberspace.

The author is currently working on several other titles in the *Goddess Series*. Keep an eye out for the release of *Gaia's Guardian, Demeter's Daughter*, and *Hestia's Healer*.

About Windstorm Creative
and our Readers' Club

Windstorm Creative was founded in 1989 to create a publishing house with author-centric ethics and cutting-edge, risk-taking innovation. Windstorm is now a company of more than ten divisions with international distribution channels that allow us to sell our books both inside the traditional systems and outside these paradigms, capitalizing on more direct delivery and non-traditional markets. As a result, our books can be found in grocery superstores as well as your favorite neighborhood bookstore, and dozens of other outlets on and off the Internet.

Windstorm is an independent press with the synergy and branding of a corporate publisher and an author royalty that's easily twice their best offer. We have continued to minimize returns without decreasing sales by publishing books that are timeless, as opposed to timely, and never back-listing.

Windstorm is constantly changing, improving, and growing. We are driven by the needs of our authors – hailing from ten different countries – and the vision of our critically-acclaimed staff. All of our books are created with the strictest of environmental protections in mind. Our approach to no-waste, no-hazard, in-house production, and stringent out-source scrutiny, assures that our goals are met whether books are printed at our own facility or an outside press.

Because of these precautions, our books cost more. And though we know that our readers support our efforts, we also understand that a few dollars can add up. This is why we began our Readers' Club. Visit our webcenter and take 20% off every title, every day. No strings. No fine print.

While you're at our site, preview or request the first chapter of any of our titles, free of charge.

Thank you for supporting an independent press.

www.windstormcreative.com
and click on Shop

See next page for Lavender Line information.

Lavender Line Series

Because all readers deserve more than pulp fiction and because lesbian authors are still under-represented in many genres. Because *diversity* is part of who we are.

Managing Editor and best-selling author Beth Mitchum heads up the Lavender Line — a series of books that can be enjoyed by all but are primarily intended for lesbian readers. Here's what Beth writes about Lavender Line:

The Lavender Line Mission Statement

To publish quality lesbian novels written by lesbian writers for lesbian readers. To encourage stories dealing with ongoing social issues surrounding gender and sexual orientation. To keep the focus on promoting the work of talented lesbian writers.

The series is growing every day. Here's just a few examples:

1000 Reasons You Might Think She is My Lover
(Angela Costa)
The Adepts of Calluna: Constellations of the Heart, Book 2
(Lesley Davis)
The Adepts of Calluna: Keeper of the Piece, Book 1
(Lesley Davis)
The Adepts of Calluna: Woven in Life's Tapestry, Book 3
(Lesley Davis)
The Amazons of Aggar: Fires of Aggar, Book 2
(Chris Anne Wolfe)
The Amazons of Aggar: Shadows of Aggar, Book 1
(Chris Anne Wolfe)
Annabel and I (Chris Anne Wolfe)
Artemisian Artist (Beth Mitchum)
Driftwood (Beth Mitchum)
Driftwood: The Music (Beth Mitchum)
Gaia's Guardian (Beth Mitchum)
The Perfect Lesbian Prenuptial Agreement (C.W. Cecil)
Roses & Thorns: Beauty and Beast Retold
(Chris Anne Wolfe)
Signs of Love (Lesléa Newman)
Still Life with Buddy (Lesléa Newman)

Find out more. Visit us at
www.windstormcreative.com/windstorm/lavender.htm